Ten years ago, August Greystone's adolescent brother was brutally murdered and dumped in Blood Pond. And the one person he is sure can identify the killer is on the run . . .

Bruce Monkton can't escape the horror of what he experienced the night his friend, Tommy Greystone, was slaughtered in front of his eyes. Although Bruce somehow survived the vicious attack, he is still fleeing from shadows, from the haunting memories and his own demons, so the last thing he wants is to come face-to-face with his greatest nightmare — the older brother of his dead boyhood crush, the man desperately seeking closure to his brother's murder.

August has given up everything, including his career as a law enforcement officer, to locate Bruce because he's sure the young man is the key to helping him find what he seeks. But can Bruce really aid August when it comes to locating the elusive killer, or will the answers to the mystery be buried forever at the bottom of Blood Pond?

This book has been previously published previously quite a few years ago. It has won many awards.

Blood Pond
Copyright © 2019 D.J. Manly
ISBN: 978-1-4874-2490-9
Cover art by Martine Jardin

Published by eXtasy Books Inc or
Devine Destinies, an imprint of eXtasy Books Inc

Look for us online at:
www.eXtasybooks.com or www.devinedestinies.com

Blood Pond
Blood Pond, Book 1

By

D.J. Manly

DEDICATION

To those who have fallen victim to the faceless killer, the one who may still be out there.

CHAPTER ONE

He was close. He could feel it. A guy who fit Monkton's' description had been held overnight at the local jail only two days ago.

"It's not really right, me telling you this." Officer Beaumont shook his head, the file between his fingers. "It's confidential really."

August studied the middle-aged cop standing behind the counter. He was a simple guy with a quiet life. The extra weight he carried around the middle testified to the fact that he wasn't used to seeing much crime in this little town. He could have been Beaumont in twenty years. "I really appreciate it," he said as he folded the faded photograph and put it back into his wallet.

"It's only because you were on the job before. What was it like being a big city cop up in Manchester?"

August tried not to think about that most days, think about what he'd left behind a few months ago. None of it mattered anymore anyway. "He didn't happen to say where he was going, did he?"

The seconds ticked by steadily on the clock overhead. The shrill ringing of a phone somewhere in the background echoed in his head, momentarily distracting the officer.

"Nope, can't say that he did. He was hungover-like. Didn't say much of anything, just looked kind of lost. I gave his personal belongings back. He didn't have much, mostly the clothes on his back. About twenty dollars and some change. That was it. We had nothing to hold him on once he'd sobered up. What's he wanted for?"

"Nothing, that I know of. Look, I saw a Bed and Breakfast up the road when I rode in. Is it open? I need to rent a room, somewhere I can sleep, get something to eat."

"Not anymore. Mr. Buckner moved away to be near his daughter in Newport, but there's Franklin House, just as you leave town. Not fancy, mind you, but Sharon is a good little cook. She'll whip you up something if you ask her."

"Is the price reasonable?" Last he'd checked, his funds were at an all-time low. He was still waiting on a payment from the insurance case he'd closed. "Let me call on over there, see what I can do." Beaumont offered.

"I'd appreciate it." He was weary and broke, and battling this depression that reached out and gripped him so hard at times, it felt as if he was gasping for breath. He would have liked nothing more than to sleep for three days, but that wasn't going to happen.

Bruce Monkton had been spotted several times in this area of Vermont. He couldn't waste too much time sleeping.

The cop was speaking on the phone to someone about the room. August walked over and studied the bulletin board. There was nothing there of interest, but then why should there be? No one knew what he looked like; no one except Monkton.

"Mr. Greystone?" Phone at his ear, Beaumont motioned to him.

August pushed his hands into the pockets of his leather jacket and walked over to the counter. "Yeah?"

"Sharon has a good room for you and a chicken in the oven. Give you a good rate, guaranteed, three meals thrown in for fifty. How's that suit you?"

"Suits me fine, thanks."

The cop spoke into the receiver a few more minutes, then hung up. "She'll be expecting you."

A few minutes later, August walked across the parking lot to his beat-up old Toyota. Every day, he prayed it wouldn't break down. It surprised him every time the engine roared to life.

He followed the road that led out of town and turned off onto an unpaved driveway which led to the Bed and Breakfast. There were no other guests, but then, it wasn't tourist season. The leaves on the trees were already beginning to drop off, and soon the snow would cover the ground.

The Franklin House was a typical New England style house with the large verandas and green shutters. The room Sharon Franklin gave him wasn't fancy, but it was clean and warm. He wolfed down the food the elderly woman prepared, apologizing every few minutes for his haste. *God, that tasted good.* He hadn't eaten like that since before his mother died. "I haven't eaten in a while."

"Young man," the grey-haired woman touched his hand, "where is it you come from, dear?"

"Manchester."

"You're a little out of the way, aren't you?"

He smiled faintly. "A little."

"Had a fellow here yesterday, came from Manchester too, I think. He was a quiet young fellow, a . . ."

August jumped up from his chair and whipped out his wallet. His fingers fumbled for a moment while the older woman watched him curiously. He pushed the picture in front of her. "Was that him? Was that the guy who was here, the one that's on the left?"

"Well . . . I . . . I . . ." She seemed flustered as she picked up the picture.

"Please, it's important."

"It's an old photograph. It's hard to make it out. This fellow was older but had the same fair hair." She put it on the table. "Needed a haircut if you ask me. These young men

3

wear their hair so long these days. In my day — "

"Please try to remember," August insisted.

"I couldn't say really." She shook her head.

"Please, take another look."

"I'd need my glasses." She stood up. "Hold on a minute."

He waited impatiently while she hunted for her glasses. If Monkton stayed here last night, right after he got out of jail, it meant he was closer to his tail than he thought. The minute she returned, he asked, "What did he say his name was? Was it, Bruce? Did he call himself Bruce?"

"No, not Bruce," she mused. "He said Clay something or other, never did tell me his family name." She lowered her voice. "I didn't know until after he'd left that he was fresh out of county jail. It was nothing to worry about. He said he drank too much. My late husband liked to tip the bottle a bit too."

August took back the photograph and slid it inside his wallet. "Did he say where he was going?"

"Well, let me think . . . yes . . . said something about going up to Canada, Montreal maybe."

August sat back down. Montreal. That would make sense somehow.

"Is that some help to you?" Mrs. Franklin asked.

"Yes. Thanks."

"What do you want him for? I mean, not my business but . . . is he kin of yours?"

"No, not kin." He picked up his fork again but didn't eat. His appetite had left him. August accepted more coffee, then went to the room, showered, and lay down on the bed.

He took out the wrinkled photograph again and stared at it like he usually did when he couldn't sleep. Two gangly, good-looking young boys in their bathing trunks; Tommy, dark-haired like himself, with their mother's dark brown eyes; Bruce Monkton, blond and tanned. He had his face turned to the side, but there was still enough of his profile to be able to make out his features. They were lying in the grass in front of Blood Pond. It was only a short bike ride away from their parents' summer cottage in the White Mountains. Bruce was on his stomach. His brother had turned his face to the camera, staring at something or at someone.

That old picture had been taped to the mirror of his brother's bureau. He'd found it on the day of the funeral. The image of his brother's face in that photo haunted him. Maybe it was just the flash of the camera or a movement in the bushes. The photograph was taken just two days before Tommy was murdered.

"Who is that boy in the picture with Tommy?" he'd asked his mother later that day after all the people had left.

He didn't get much of an answer. A few days later when he asked her again, she said his name was Bruce. He and his mother had rented a cottage across the lake for the summer.

"Who took the picture, Mom?" he'd persisted. "Did Tommy mention who had taken this picture?"

There was an ominous silence. A chill went up his back when his mother looked at him and whimpered, "God, August, I don't know."

He'd given that picture to the police, but it had been taken with a cheap Polaroid camera and wasn't of any use to them. At the end, August had taken it back.

It was after midnight when sleep finally claimed him. He awoke off and on, thinking he really should head out to Montreal, but sleep pulled him down, again and again, pinning him to the mattress. When he opened his eyes in the wee hours of the morning, this time, he was in a panic. He thought he'd forgotten where that photo was. What had he done with the picture? He searched blindly on the bed in the dark as his forehead broke out into a sweat. He leaned over and tried to turn on the reading lamp. It fell unbroken to the carpeted floor.

He picked up the lamp and switched it on, suddenly spotting the photograph lying on the faded blue carpet beside the bed. He reached out for it, picked it up and slid it back into his wallet again.

He forced himself out of bed. He would have liked to have showered again, but he didn't want to wake up Mrs. Franklin.

Dressing, he left the money he owed and wrote her a brief note, thanking her for her hospitality. In the car, he set his GPS for Montreal, cranked up the radio to some tune by CCR, and spun out of the yard.

It was freezing in the truck. The rain was coming down in sheets, getting heavier the closer they got to Montreal. It was cold rain, mixed with ice, and the driver hadn't bothered to slow his pace at all since it had begun.

"*Ay*," he said, his French accent seeming more pronounced than it had been an hour ago, "nervous, *toi*?"

"No, no, I'm fine," Bruce told him, but his hands gripped the sides of the passenger seat. It was worse sitting so high up. He felt as if the rain would suddenly burst through the window and swallow him whole. "Really coming down." When the driver didn't appear to understand that idiom, Bruce pointed to the windshield. "The rain, man. It's really . . . ah . . . *fort*. Strong!"

He laughed and shrugged as if he'd seen it all before. "Okay, okay." He waved. "Big, me. I big with . . . have big truck!"

Bruce smiled faintly and tried to relax. He knew a big truck like this could hug the road quite well. He'd hitched a ride in plenty of them, and even in the worst snow storms, they'd barrel on through while other smaller vehicles were relegated to the ditch. But it didn't take much to get him stressed out.

He'd gotten lucky with Jean-Pierre. The transport driver had seen him hitchhiking near the truck stop and pulled over. He wasn't supposed to take anyone in the cab for insurance purposes, but he wanted to practice his English. And amazingly enough, that's all he wanted, no blowjob, or screw in the back of the cab. That was a relief.

On the way to Montreal, Jean-Pierre talked about his kids, showed him pictures of a son a few years younger than Bruce and a grown daughter with two babies. His wife's picture was pinned up above his visor; a plump woman with a generous smile. Bruce almost envied him.

"Why you go to Montreal?" he asked him as the Champlain Bridge came into view.

"I don't know," Bruce said. "I need a change I guess."

"You need change . . . what for, young like you? I need change." He laughed. "I'm old man."

Bruce looked out the window. He could see a huge Ferris wheel and, beyond that, a huge metal globe. "Expo, right?" he looked at the driver.

"Um, before you, *jeune homme.*"

"Were you there?"

"*Oui*, nineteen . . . how you say that, six and seven?"

"nineteen sixty-seven," Bruce told him.

"It was good, fun. I was like you, *jeune homme.*
You meet a person here, family, *amie*?"

"No. I'll be okay. Where are you taking all the frozen stuff, you're transporting?"

"*Entrepot*, ah . . . house store?"

"Warehouse."

"That's it. Where you go?"

"Can you leave me downtown . . . ah . . . *Centreville*?"

"Sure?"

"Sure." Bruce nodded.

The rain had slowed, but not much. Bruce threw the hood of his sweater up over his head. If he stayed here through the winter, he'd have to find a coat, and some boots too. He hoped he could get a job, something that didn't require identification papers. He had no visa to work in Canada.

Jean-Pierre seemed reluctant to let him leave. He offered to buy him breakfast at a fast food place, and they ate in the parking lot, gulping big cups of coffee and munching on sausage and egg sandwiches.

"You live in Montreal, Jean-Pierre?" Bruce asked him, scrunching up the garbage and putting it into a bag.

"Dorval," he said. "I go home by," he checked his watch, "ten this morning. I leave truck. My car is at the ..." he paused and grinned, "waring house."

"You get home at ten ... and it's warehouse."

"Right. *Merde.* warehouse, and get home. I don't take out the box at the ... the warehouse."

"Ah, that's good," Bruce told him. He looked around. The street sign said Ste. Catherine. "I'm going to get going, Jean-Pierre," he said. "Thanks for the food and the ride. You take care." He held out his hand.

The trucker shook it. "*Toi aussi,*" he said. "*Salute,* Clay!"

"*Salute.*" Bruce opened the door and dropped down to the pavement.

He pulled the sweater around him. The rain had slacked, but it was cold. He could feel the wind coming off the St. Lawrence River. There was no sun, but the dawn had broken. The stores along Ste. Catherine hadn't opened yet, but the restaurants were already serving breakfast.

He kept his hands in his pocket as he walked, not sure where he was going. He just knew he needed to move. Maybe he could lose himself here on this island where people from many different ethnic groups appeared to live together peacefully. Maybe *he* was here too, waiting tables in a restaurant on Prince Arthur, playing music in the gay village . . . just watching . . . waiting . . .

An hour later, he sat in a coffee shop near McGill University on Sherbrooke, looking through the wanted ads in *The Gazette*. A few students sat around a corner table, knapsacks at their feet, drinking cappuccino.

After the coffee, he had twelve dollars left in his pocket, hardly enough to get him a room for the night. It was cold, and he wasn't looking forward to spending the night in a park, but he would if he had to.

Busboy, waiter, bartender, trucker, dancer . . . All of them would require identification. None of them would earn him money right away or give him a place to sleep tonight.

He finished his coffee and left the café. He headed back to Ste. Catherine Street and then made for the village and those distinctive bars and restaurants that lay between Papineau and Berri, marked by the rainbow flag hanging over Beaudry Metro station. The Club Sandwich, the Cabaret Chez Mado, Le Parking, and a number of other clubs, saunas, and restaurants all vied for the patronage of the gay and lesbian population. Last time he was here it had given him comfort, shelter, and a job.

When he climbed up the familiar carpeted steps of the empty club, the first person he saw was Karl. Bruce was happy to see him standing there, wiping glasses with a towel, and even happier when Karl recognized him. "Clay!" he shouted. He threw down the towel and came to plant an affectionate kiss on both cheeks. "I never thought you'd come back. How long has it been?"

"Almost two years," Bruce told him. "How are you?"

"Fantastic. Stephen and I got married." He showed him his gold band.

"Congratulations. Karl, you wouldn't have a job for me, would you? I'd do anything."

"Anything?" He chuckled. "Don't let some of the horny old queens in here hear you say that."

Bruce smiled, nervously entwining his fingers. "I don't want to sleep outside tonight."

"Come to the bar. What are you drinking?" Karl asked, setting a glass in front of him.

"Ah, just Coke, okay?"

Karl eyed him. "Are you on the wagon? I seem to remember you tying on a couple when you were here."

"Yeah, I wanted to say sorry about that, and about the damage. I—"

Karl poured him some Coke. "Never mind. You dry for real?"

"I'm trying. I can't guarantee anything."

Karl sighed. "I don't know what I can do, my friend. Stephen was pretty pissed about what happened . . . and when you fell off the stage that time. We did take a risk hiring you, since you're illegal and everything. Inspectors are strict now, especially in the village. You know."

"I have nowhere else to go." *Nowhere to hide, do you?*

Karl nodded. "You eaten?"

"Yeah, this morning."

"Well, now it's afternoon. I've got some sandwiches in the fridge. Chicken or tuna?"

"Doesn't matter."

"I'll be right back," Karl said.

Bruce sipped his Coke, eyeing the bottles of liquor that lined the back of the bar. He turned away and scanned the large room. It was a small bar by most standards, holding a hundred at the most. It had a certain class, white tablecloths on the tables, candles, and they served some fast foods, as well as drinks.

The stage was upfront, a disc jockey station to the left, and a small dance floor to the right.

The strippers were usually hand-picked and gorgeous. There was a cover charge or used to be. Karl and Stephen had done some redecorating; wallpaper with statues of Adonis or was it, David—he could never tell which—adorned the walls, and the trim was lavender of course.

"Here you go." Karl handed him a sandwich.

Bruce turned around and took it. "Thanks. I like what you've done."

"Stephen's the artistic one. Great, isn't it?"

"Yeah. Still charge to get in?"

"You bet. We're full every night too."

"And the dancers . . . do you . . . can you give me a spot, maybe advance me a few dollars so that I can get room?" He knew Karl had a soft spot for him. When Karl gave him a job last time, he and Stephen were going through a hard time. Karl had fucked him one night in the stock room after an argument. Bruce didn't remember it much. He'd been drunk most of the time anyway. But he'd been counting on the fact that maybe Karl remembered.

Karl reached over and covered his hand with his. "Look, I'll talk to Stephen. He can't deny you really could bring in the crowd. And if you promise to—"

"I will," Bruce said quickly. "I'll be good. You have my word."

"Look, we got an empty room upstairs. No one's staying in it. Why don't you go on up, take a shower? Get some sleep before the crowd comes in. Let me break it to Stephen before he sees you, okay?"

"I don't know how I can repay you, Karl."

"No payment necessary. I'll give you a spot on the weekend, okay, see if I can't advance you a few dollars in the meantime."

"I can clean up, serve food."

Karl nodded. "You got a winter coat?"

"No."

"I'll see what I can dig up. Clay?"

Bruce looked at him. "Yeah?"

"I really hoped you'd have your life together by now. What's going on with you? You're smart and good-looking. You shouldn't be back here. Maybe you'll tell me finally what you're running from?"

Bruce finished the Coke and left his half-eaten sandwich on the bar. "I'm not running from anything, really. I just can't seem to catch a break, that's all."

Karl nodded. "Come on, I'll take you upstairs."

The room was small, sparsely furnished, but it had its own bathroom and shower. There were clean towels and linen. Karl handed him a key. "Let me know if you need something, okay?"

"You've been more than kind, man. Thanks. I promise not to piss off Stephen this time."

Karl nodded as he left, closing the door behind him.

Bruce stripped off his clothes and got into the shower. The water took a few minutes to get warm, but it felt incredible. He stepped out and wrapped himself in a towel, staring down at his underwear, full of holes. He threw them in the sink along with his socks, and washed them, stringing them over the shower rod to dry.

He lay down on the bed, trying to remember the last time his head had touched a pillow. In his mind, he saw trees, trees, and more trees. There were strange noises overhead, the cracking of branches under feet. Breathing, hard and loud, hushed sobs, his feet cut and bleeding. Oh God, oh God, oh God . . . please . . . please . . . scrambling up to the side of the road . . . the loud horn blared, the truck almost jackknifing . . . its wheels screeching . . . burning on the pavement . . . and he kept running, across the road and back into the trees, surrounded by darkness. A face . . . a large silhouette hovering over him. A bizarre mask with a laconic grin. Bizarre eyes . . . crazed . . . peering down at him . . . the sharp glint of steel. He was underwater now, his lungs burning.

Bruce gasped, struggling to breathe. He sat up straight and searched the darkness for any sound or movement. He drew up his knees and hugged them to his body. With his eyes closed, he rocked back and forth. "It's all right, it's all right, it's all right," he said, over and over. "He can't find you. He doesn't know where you are. He doesn't know where you are."

But I do.

August opened his laptop in an internet café. He checked his email, relieved to see that finally the money from his last job had been deposited into his PayPal account. He transferred it immediately, aware it would take at least three days before he could access it at a bank machine.

He brought up the Google map and located the gay village. The last time he'd traced Monkton here, he'd just left a job at some strip club on Ste. Catherine Street. The owner of the club had been livid when August had shown him his picture. "The guy wrecked my club, went nuts one night after closing and broke a lot of stuff, left me with over two thousand bucks in damages. He was a drunk, couldn't control his drinking, and fucking crazy. Damn shame though. The clients loved him."

The map reminded him of where this place was. He googled Le Spot, and according to the website, it was still there. So were the owners, Stephen and Karl. He had no reason to think Bruce went back there after what he'd done except that he was an illegal. Chances were that he'd end up dancing in one of these places again for cash. So, if he wasn't at Le Spot, maybe these guys could point him in the right direction.

He finished his coffee, ordered a muffin to go, and found his car again; five blocks down. Damn hard to find parking in this city. He was tempted to take the Metro.

Driving down Ste. Catherine Street was slow and laborious. It was seven o'clock on a Thursday night, and the stores were open until nine. Jaywalking seemed to be perfected to an art in this city. He ate his muffin as he drove and opened his window a crack, watching the swarm of people everywhere.

When he saw the rainbow flag, he looked for parking and luckily found a tight spot on a side street. He got out, pulled his jacket around him, and walked back up to the main drag. The restaurants were full, and so were the stores. Bookstores and sex shops featuring gay erotica in the windows gave people pause as they strolled along.

August checked for the bar at every corner, remembering that it had been upstairs on the second floor, a little out-of-the-way place that was packed the night he visited.

He passed it twice, realizing that they'd changed the sign from white to purple and the fonts on the lettering were fancier. He paused at the bottom as two men brushed past him. They looked back at him and smiled. "Hey, baby," one said. "Aren't you sweet."

Sweet? He'd never been called that before. He nodded at them, and one of the guys held open the door.

"Don't be shy." One man gave him a wink.

August laughed. "Okay," he said and followed him in.

"What's your name?" the guy asked as the other guy wandered off. He was a slim fellow, probably around thirty years old, nice looking.

"August." He smiled. It seemed so far away, even the

thought of flirting with someone again.

"This must be my lucky night, August. You're gorgeous. Can I buy you a drink?"

"Maybe later." Right now, he had more important things to take care of.

He looked around the room as he walked in. It was already half full. August spotted that Stephen guy near the bar and walked over. "Mr. Lachance?"

Stephen Lachance turned around, a tall, well-built Jamaican man with a beautiful, rich accent. He narrowed his eyes, then smiled. "*Oui?*"

"I don't know if you remember me but —"

"*Cheri,*" he ran his gaze over August, "I'd have to be blind not to remember a man as good-looking as you. What can I help you with?"

"I wanted to ask about someone who worked for you a while back. I believe he went by the name of Clay. I have reason to believe he may be back in Montreal."

"Clay?" He snorted. "Not in my place, he isn't. The guy is a headcase. Loco." He made a circle with his finger round his temple.

"Any idea who may be hiring dancers in the village without . . . well . . ."

"Illegals? Ha, take your pick, baby. They all do it."

"Can you maybe suggest where to start?"

"Come here." He motioned and led him over to the bar. "Relax, sit down, have a drink, on the house." He poured him a whiskey. "You look stressed right out." August thanked him and took a swig.

"Whatever obsession you got with this guy, give it up man. It's going to kill you. He's cute and all but —"

"It's not like that," August told him.

"I've heard that before, sweet man. But if you haven't found him in all this time, he doesn't want to be found. And you can't reform 'em, honey, I know."

"I don't want to reform him," he replied impatiently. "I don't want to fuck him either. I just need him to tell me who murdered my brother."

Stephen Lachance's eyes bugged out of his head.

August drained his glass and put it back down on the bar. He hadn't realized that his voice had gotten so loud. People looked over at the bar curiously. He stood and lowered his voice. His hand shook. "I'm sorry. Look, if you don't want to help me, then don't. Even if it takes fifty fucking years, I'll find him."

He was halfway down the stairs when Stephen Lachance caught up to him. He grabbed his arm and looked him in the eye. "Give me a number where I can reach you.

If I see him, I'll call you, okay?"

August pulled out one of his business cards. "It's my cell phone. Don't worry if I don't answer; leave a message."

He nodded, looking at the card. "Okay. Try to relax, man."

"I'll relax," he said, running down the stairs, "when I find Bruce Monkton."

CHAPTER TWO

B ruce knew Stephen was angry. He seemed to be having a hard time retaining his composure, and several times he took Karl aside and engaged him in a lively, yet subdued, discussion.

The expression on Karl's face was pained, and Bruce couldn't help but feel guilty for causing problems between them. But he didn't know what else to do.

"Look, if he wants me gone, I'll go," he told Karl. He had been sitting quietly at the end of the bar for the last half hour, fighting off several men who assumed he was there looking for a pick-up.

Karl stood close to him, his expression softening. "He'll get over it. I told him you'd pitch in tomorrow night, work for nothing." He winced. "We're going to be shorthanded tomorrow night, and Monday is Thanksgiving."

Bruce narrowed his eyes. "It's only October."

"Yes, love, but our Thanksgiving isn't at the same time as yours."

"Oh, I forgot, and sure," Bruce piped up enthusiastically. "I'll work all weekend for free, as long as I can stay here and get a bite or two."

"It's a deal." Karl looked relieved. "I'm telling you, that will please him, show good faith."

The disc jockey announced the next dancer, in both French and English. "Here he is, guys, beautiful Danny . . . Danny . . . le beauty!"

A slender young man with long reddish-brown hair got

17

up to dance to "I Want to Know What Love Is," and the packed room applauded loudly, whistling when Danny slid his hand into his jock strap and rubbed his shaft seductively.

Two muscle-bound guys in jocks served drinks to the clients. Bruce didn't recognize either one of them. But they came and went in this business, moving around from club to club.

Stephen served drinks at the bar, and Karl greeted and seated the customers. By two in the morning, there was standing room only. Bruce gave up his stool to a middle-aged, bespectacled man and went behind the bar to help Karl wash glasses in the sink.

Stephen didn't acknowledge him at all, but he seemed to have gotten over his initial anger; he was having a good time socializing with the customers. The other dancers took their turns on the stage, whipping off their jock straps and running their hands over their own naked, shiny bodies.

Karl made a few comments about one of the dancer's oversized cock, and Bruce found himself laughing a little. He'd always liked Karl, and he could almost imagine being with someone, sharing little jokes, and curling up to them in bed. *Almost.* But it could never be. He could never stay in one place that long. Even now, despite the laughter and the ambiance, there was this underlying tension, this coil in his gut that caused him to search the faces of those who approached him. *Is that him? Has he come for me already?*

Who was Plato's lover? What year did Rome fall?

Who won . . . who did . . . who said . . .

I don't know. I don't know. God . . . help me . . . I don't fucking know!

"Bruce?"

He blinked and found himself looking into Karl's eyes.

"You're shaking all over. Are you all right?"

Bruce looked down to see that he'd dropped a glass in the sink. "I'm sorry, I . . ."

"Your hand is bleeding. Come on. Let me get you a bandage."

He watched the blood drip into the sink for a second. Blood. All that blood in pools. More blood . . . draining away . . . *Die . . . let him die . . . stop the pain. I don't know any of the answers. Please, God, stop this!* "I need a drink," he said abruptly.

"No, Bruce," Karl said, bringing him into the back room. He took down the first aid kit. "You promised. No drinking."

"Please, God, Karl, just one," he pleaded, "or something for my nerves." He reached into his pocket and drew out a plastic pill bottle. He hadn't had his prescription filled for Ativan in months. "Do you have something that can just calm me down a little?"

"Maybe, I don't know." Karl took his hand and cleaned the wound with an antiseptic swab. "What's got you so up-tight? Stephen is okay now."

"I don't know. I have this condition," he swallowed, looking around, "I just get this way." They'd fucked in this room, this tiny room where Karl kept the first aid kit and the safe with all the money. It seemed smaller suddenly, dark. He felt his throat clog up. "Can we get out of here now? I'm feeling a little . . ."

Karl put a bandage around his finger. "Okay, should be fine."

Bruce felt a little better when they were back in the main room, surrounded by people and music. The crowd had thinned a bit; the dancers were finished. Some men danced together, trying to entice a stranger to spend a little quiet time with them somewhere later.

"Where's Stephen?" Karl asked.

Bruce started to clean up the broken glass. "Don't know."

August didn't want to sleep in his car, but it seemed like it was shaping up that way. He'd been to several clubs that night and didn't see anyone resembling Bruce Monkton. None of the bar owners had seen him either.

He'd had several invitations and the way he felt now he was more than tempted to accept one of them. A good fuck in the back room might be just what he needed to clear his head. He wasn't sure if he was up for much more than that really. That muffin he'd eaten was long gone. He was hungry and exhausted.

He walked into one last bar around closing time and showed the picture to the bartender, a handsome Italian with incredible eyes, not to mention biceps. "You know," he said, "when you walked in that door, my heart flip-flopped. I thought I was going into cardiac arrest. Where you from, beautiful man?"

He put the picture back into his wallet. He couldn't help him, at least not with Bruce Monkton. "What is it with guys up here? I've been called sweet, and pretty, and beautiful. Don't you use handsome and good-looking anymore?"

"Naw, you're way beyond handsome, sweetheart. My cock is going into overdrive. You're not from here. You got an accent. American, right?"

"Right."

"Oh, sweetie, that's what my cock is doing." He leaned across the bar. "It's standing up for the 'Star-Spangled Banner.'"

For some reason, that struck August funny. He laughed. "That must be painful."

"Oh, now I'm in love," he said.

"You know what I think?" he said, deciding to flirt back a little. "I think you're a real smooth talker, and that you probably fall in love every night."

"Well," he winked, "not every night. Are you in town long?"

"I don't know yet. That depends." He looked around.

"Be still my heart. Maybe I could convince you to stick around for the rest of my life."

He smiled at the bartender. He really wished that it was that simple, that he could just wait around with this guy until closing and go somewhere where they could fuck each other's brains out. And he could just forget for a little while. Forget. Forget that he didn't get back for Tommy's birthday that year. He remembered calling him that night.

I'll be down soon, Tommy. We'll do something, okay?

You owe me big time. I want a big gift. A car.

Dream on!

He did go home though, home to Tommy's funeral, but he never did see his brother again, not even in the coffin because . . . because . . .

"Hey, gorgeous, where did you go? I lost you, man."

He looked up at the bartender. "Sorry. What did you say?"

"I'm losing my touch. I said I get off in twenty minutes. Want to go somewhere, get something to eat?"

"Ah, sure," he said with a nod. He might as well. He had no place to sleep anyway. And maybe for a few hours, he'd be distracted, and the pain would be forgotten.

They walked together to an all-night sandwich place down the street. It was full. August studied the menu, trying to determine if he could afford anything on it.

The bartender, whose name was Gino, reached over suddenly and took the menu from him. He closed it and put it back in the holder. "Don't worry about it. It's on me."

"No, I can't let you—"

"Listen, I'll take it out in trade," he said then burst out laughing when he saw August's expression. "I'm kidding. A kiss would be nice but not necessary. Don't be so serious. I'm the one who did the inviting. Besides, I know what's good here. You like smoked meat . . . pastrami?"

"Sure."

"They make it great here."

The waiter came over. "Hey, Gino."

"Hey, hot stuff. Look, two of your pastrami plates, extra lean, and two Cokes." He looked at August, who nodded. "Big tip if you get it here fast."

He laughed. "What kind of tip?"

"Get outta here." Gino gave him a shove.

August leaned back in his seat. "You come here often I see."

"Yeah, every night after work. I love the food, and the waiters aren't bad either. So, what's your story, or is mystery part of your appeal? You want coffee?"

"Sure, but at least let me pay for that."

"You got it." He motioned to the cute waiter.

"Caffeine!"

"Coming up," he hollered back.

As they sat stirring their coffee, Gino asked him again about his life. "You don't have to tell me. The mystery thing really works for you. I'm hyperventilating over here. God, you're hot."

August shook his head, smiling. "And you're a piece of work."

"I am. Wait until you try me on for size."

August laughed. It felt good to laugh, to talk to someone. He spent far too much time alone. "I'm looking for someone."

"I figured that. That picture is pretty dated. Shouldn't you give it up now?"

"It's not like that."

"Weren't you one of those guys in that picture?"

He swallowed hard. It was ten years ago. Would Tommy look that much like him today? He'd be almost twenty-five. Would he be tall like him, muscular with broad shoulders? He had the same black hair, but Tommy's eyes had been brown, not dark blue like his. "No," he managed. "It's not me. It's my brother."

"And the other one, the one you asked me about, the sweet little Twink? Who is he?"

He sipped his coffee. It was hot, and it burned his mouth. He felt uncomfortable talking about this, but he needed to say it. "He was with my brother when . . . when he was killed."

"Oh . . . I'm sorry. I didn't mean to . . . Shit. Was it an accident?"

"No. It was murder." He raised his head.

Gino's startled eyes filled with horror. "I'm sorry."

"Can we change the subject?"

He nodded. "Sure."

They ate their sandwiches, and Gino told him a bit about himself. He was part owner of the club, and his partner had been his former lover, but it was over. He was saving his money to buy his partner out and longed for the day when he could run it on his own.

As they left the sandwich shop, Gino made no secret of the fact that he wanted him. The sun would soon be up, and it was chilly outside. "I live over the bar," he said. "It's not big, but it's home. You can crash if you want. No strings."

August looked in those eyes and saw so many things, things he'd scarcely dared even think about, desire, hope, need, life. And suddenly, he didn't want to be alone.

Gino waited for his answer, his expression tense, filled with anticipation.

"Sounds good," August said. "Lead the way."

The Montreal streets were quiet. An early morning frost

coated the grass, and the sky looked menacing. Before they got back to the club, the rain had started to fall, cold and unforgiving. They climbed the winding back steps to the apartment above, and Gino opened the door. "You don't have allergies to cats, do you?"

"No."

Just as they stepped in, a beautiful, white Angora cat wound around his feet, crying. August reached down and patted her head.

"Hungry," Gino explained, pouring out some food into a bowl and changing the water.

"She's beautiful."

"He. His name is Minx."

August grinned. "Aw, beautiful males."

The kitchen was small but well equipped, a little messy but clean. There were dishes in the dish rack and a lot of newspapers scattered on the table.

Gino put down the food, and Minx went right for it. He motioned to August to follow, and August walked into the living room. A huge sofa and a big flat screen television were the only things in the room. It was small, but it looked cozy.

"Just three rooms," Gino said, sitting on the sofa. "One bedroom, but if you . . . I mean . . . You can have the sofa. You don't have to sleep on the . . ." He was picking at the arm of the chair a little.

August took off his jacket and walked over to the sofa. He placed one leg between Gino's knees.

Gino looked up at him.

"I have no intention of sleeping on the sofa." He met his gaze and then pulled off his t-shirt. "You mind if I take a shower first?"

"It's right there." Gino pointed to the door next to the bedroom.

August reached down and took his arm. He pulled him to his feet. "How about you join me?"

Gino's tongue came out and licked his lips. He smiled. "Need some help finding the soap?" His body leaned into August's.

"Something like that."

Gino placed his hands, on August's naked chest. "I'll do what I can."

August bent his head down and kissed him gently on the mouth then headed to the bathroom.

Gino was right behind him. "Guess I can start by helping you with these clothes."

August stood still while Gino undid his jeans with shaking fingers. "God, you're so beautiful."

"I'm beginning to like that." August smiled, suddenly pushing aside his hands and taking down the rest of the zipper. "You're shaking like a leaf. At this rate, we'll . . ." He trailed off as Gino took off his own shirt, kicked off his shoes, and then his pants, and underwear.

"Jesus."

The guys' body was a masterpiece, a playground, and his cock was indeed standing up.

"You like?" He smiled.

August pulled him into his arms, ran his hands over his back, his ass. "Damn, you got a great ass. I want to fuck you."

He chuckled. "What about the shower?"

"Right," August muttered, releasing him. He watched while Gino turned on the water. His hands reached out to caress Gino's perfect, round ass. August was hard as hell, and he guessed that he'd been that way awhile.

"I got lube and condoms in the medicine cabinet," Gino said, opening the door.

August took them and put them on the side of the tub

then he stepped into the shower and pulled him in with him. Gino closed the shower curtain and pressed August against the tile. He lifted his arms and held them up against the wall with one hand while he kissed his throat and his chest, tongued his nipples. The other hand stroked his cock and massaged his testicles.

August closed his eyes. He let his head loll to one side, allowing himself to feel. *Pleasure.* Oh God, it had been so long. He felt guilty, but that was all right. Guilty for being alive, for feeling pleasure but umm . . . yeah . . . it was okay. Make it hurt. He wanted it to hurt.

He gasped as Gino urged him to turn around, his hard cock slapping the tile as Gino got to his knees. The water cascaded over them, and Gino's tongue delved deep inside his ass. *Jesus . . . yes . . . yesssss . . . God . . . mercy . . . mercy . . .* . He humped the tile and then turned, clutching Gino's hard body to his as Gino reached for the lube.

August took it from him. He reached around Gino, his fingers coated with lube, and delved deep within, pushing and hooking, and forcing a scream from his lips as Gino's cum trickled down his shaft, wetting August's thigh.

"Fuck, yeah . . . yeah," he grunted as August turned him to face the wall and pulled his ass forward, bending him some at the waist. He continued to use his fingers, exploring deep inside of him, finding that place that coaxed deep groans from Gino's lips. "Fuck me!"

He ripped open the condom and rolled it onto his dick. One hand roamed Gino's body, mauling his nipples, his cock, and his testicles. He positioned his cockhead at his opening and pushed past the first set of muscles. He squeezed Gino's shaft hard and then plunged deeper inside of him.

"God, you're so big, so thick . . . God . . . yeah . . . that's it. Take me. Take me. August, you're so fucking beautiful!"

He almost lost his mind for a minute. He was lost inside of his lover, the pleasure around his shaft, in his balls, the pressure, the tension . . . Oh yeah . . . yeah . . . The release made his body spasm all over. He grunted a few times, held the hard body against his and kissed his neck.

"Gino," he whispered. "Gino."

He needed to know that he was real, that he was holding a real live person in his arms. "I'm inside you," he whispered. "Do you feel me?"

"Oh yeah," he grunted. "I feel you, baby."

He laid his head on Gino's back, resting for a moment. He stroked Gino's cock a little and felt Gino coming back to life.

"My God, baby, again?" Gino laughed a little.

"Yeah, please." August licked his lips.

"You're a horny gay boy's dream."

He laughed. He felt the need grow inside of him again. "I'm alive," he whispered.

Gino glanced back at him then pressed his mouth to his. They kissed deeply for moment, the passion growing again, intense. "Oh Jesus," Gino moaned. "Um, um." He reached up and turned off the water as August began to lightly twist his nipples. "We're going to drown. Come to bed." He separated himself from August and threw him a towel. "Grab the rubbers, the lube."

August wiped his hair and his chest, staring down at his rock-hard cock. He threw the towel aside and picked up the supplies.

Gino was lying on the bed. The sun was up now, and the room was brightly lit. August raked his gaze over Gino's naked body, his hard cock, and his muscular thighs.

His knees were bent, legs open. He was ready.

August spread some more lube on his fingers and crawled between Gino's legs. Gino grabbed his head and kissed him hotly again. August ran his oily fingers over the bartender's diamond hard nipples, pinching and playing with them a little as Gino reached out and fondled August's cock. "How big is it hard? Did you ever measure?" he asked him, leaning over and pressing his lips to it.

"I don't know," August said, rubbing his thumbs over Gino's nipples then leaning down and nibbling at one of them. "Seven inches I think."

"Jesus. It feels like ten. It's oh God . . . What are you doing to me, baby?"

August pushed him back down. He continued his assault on his nipples while the other hand went under his ass. "I'm going to fingerfuck your ass for a while, and then I'm going to use your beautiful mouth."

"Mmm, talk dirty to me, baby." He laughed and moved his tongue into August's mouth. Their tongues danced for a few minutes, and then Gino cried out as August's fingers found that pleasure zone.

Gino was pleading to be fucked, but August was in no hurry this time. He withdrew his fingers, dragged Gino's head to the side of the bed, and then moved around to the side. He slid the head of his cock over Gino's lips for a few minutes while Gino licked the pre-cum with his tongue. "You taste so sweet. Give me that cock. Let me show you a few deepthroat tricks I know."

August smiled at him and massaged his jaw then Gino opened his lips, and August lowered the head of his cock into his mouth.

Gino wasn't kidding about tricks. He could deepthroat like a pro, and August was on the verge of coming when he urged Gino to release his cock. "If you want to get fucked, you better—"

Gino immediately let him go and got up on the bed on all fours. August got behind him and took him hard and fast. They both came, gasping, completely drenched and totally worn out.

Gino snuggled up to him on the pillow as August closed his eyes. "Man, I should have bought you two sandwiches," he teased.

August smiled, mumbling something, and fell into the darkness.

Where are you? Where are you, August? Why did you leave me all alone? Why didn't you come for my birthday? You let him hurt me. He hurt me bad . . . . he hurt me . . . August, help me. Happy birthday to you, Happy birthday to you. Happy birthday, dear dead Tommy. Happy birthday to you . . .

Bruce stood there, half asleep in front of the toilet. He didn't know what time it was. He just knew he couldn't sleep. Even the liquor he'd snuck from the bar at closing time didn't help him. He drank half a bottle of gin, and instead of sleeping, he lay there wide awake, as if in a coma, hearing and thinking and seeing everything. *Please, God, let me sleep. Give me one night without seeing those eyes . . . without seeing . . . the blood.*

I'm here.

He looked around. Nothing but silence. "Leave me alone," he whispered, rubbing his eyes. It was light outside. Nothing could hurt him in the daytime. He checked the door. It was locked. He huddled down under the blanket. *Sleep. Sleep.* But he hadn't any pills left, nothing to relax him, or get rid of the voice in his head, and a half a bottle of gin wasn't enough to knock him out. It was just enough to give him one hell of a hangover.

He had to dispose of the bottle before Karl found out. It was only half a bottle. He wouldn't miss it. He thought of a song his mother used to sing him when he was a baby. *Hush, little baby, don't say a word. Mama's going to buy you a mocking bird . . . So, hush little baby, don't you cry. Daddy loves you, and so do I. Daddy loves you, and so do I.*

Hey, kid. Want to see him scream? What would you do to stop him from screaming?

Anything.

Anything? Get over here. Come here. Come on.

Take your clothes off. All of them. On your knees. Go on. Do it.

Please don't. Don't do that to him. Don't hurt him. Don't . . . don't . . .

He sat up, his mouth dry.

Why don't you kill yourself, kill us?

He didn't really know why he didn't do it. He'd certainly thought about it often enough. After it happened, he'd dwelled on it for months. It was all he thought about. Somehow, he couldn't do it. He couldn't let that bastard have him too. Why did he kill Tommy? Why not him first? Why did he make him sit there and watch, play contestant in his evil little game show, witness the horror?

What is the queen's middle name? What chapter of the Bible talks about the resurrection? Why is the fucking sky blue?

Bruce covered his ears. "I don't know," he whispered. "I'm sorry, Tommy, I'm so sorry, I just didn't know."

CHAPTER THREE

"This was a one-night thing, wasn't it?" Gino asked him. August sat at the table and drank down the coffee Gino offered. "I'm sorry. Yeah."

"*You're* sorry?"

The sink faucet dripped steadily. A pan coated with leftover scrambled eggs sat on the stove. The kitchen was shrouded in splotchy shadows.

August reached over and took his hand. "You wouldn't want me anyway. I'm not good for much."

"Oh, baby, that's not true. Why would you say that?"

"I can't love anyone. I . . ." He bit his lower lip to keep it from trembling. "I have to do some shit first. And if I ever find him, maybe I can get some answers, maybe I can put this to rest for good. I don't know."

"You blame yourself, don't you?"

"Yes."

"Why? Tell me what happened?"

"Why would I do that, so that it can fucking haunt you too? You're better off not knowing, my friend."

"I'm a big boy. Let me be the judge of that. You said your brother was murdered. Do you know by whom?"

"No, but the police suspect it was a serial killer, the same killer who killed several other boys in other parts of New England. It was always boys between the ages of fourteen and sixteen. He would hold onto them for a few days; rape them, torture them, and then cut them up into pieces. He would throw the head into a lake, or pond somewhere, separated from the body. He liked to operate in cottage country, where there were trees and places he could hide."

"And they had no leads on this guy?"

"Nothing. He left no trace. But in my brother's case, there was a witness."

"Witness? You mean this bastard had an accomplice?"

"No. My brother had a friend, the one I showed you in the picture. He was someone who rented a cottage near us that summer. I'm sure he was taken by this creep at the same time, but he got away."

"Why didn't he come forward, go to the cops?"

"I don't know. All I know is I found his mother. I don't think she even reported him missing. The police were sure Tommy was alone."

"Honey, maybe they were right. Chances are no one could have escaped this maniac."

"Look at the picture." August dragged it out and put it on the table. "You see my brother's expression? Someone took that picture of them that summer, and Tommy was surprised. He didn't expect it. It's all woods there around Blood Pond, and that maniac was lurking in those woods. He was watching them, Gods know for how long. I think he wanted them both, and I think since they were together all the time, he took them both."

"Blood Pond," Gino echoed.

"Yeah. That's where he dumped my little brother or . . . what was left of him."

"My God."

August put the picture back into his pocket and sat down again.

"August, even if it is true, even if you find this Bruce, and he can tell you what this killer looks like; what then? This is like ten years ago. What if he didn't see him, not really, or he's blocked it out?"

"I have to know." August looked over at the dripping sink suddenly. "I just have to know."

"How long have you been tracking him?"

"Off and on for three years. I came here almost two years ago, took time off from work. But he'd gone, had some trouble at the bar where he was working. For the last six weeks, I've been right behind him."

"What about your job?"

"I've been picking up work here and there."

A little while later, he grabbed his jacket and took out his phone. It was flashing. He opened it up. Nothing. His phone card had run out. Damn. He had messages he couldn't get to. He wondered if one of the people he'd spoken to yesterday had something for him.

"What's wrong?" Gino asked as August put on his coat.

"Nothing. My phone is dead, that's all."

"Use mine."

"No, it's my messages I can't get to. I'll get a phone card."

"If you need money, I . . ."

"Gino," August turned to him and put his hands on his shoulders, "you've been great, but I can't let you do anything more for me. I have money coming in soon. I just have to be patient. I got enough for the next couple of days."

"Where you going to sleep?"

"I'll find something."

"Come here and—"

"No. I can't impose on you like that."

"It's no imposition. Please, promise me you'll come back if you—"

He kissed him gently on the mouth. "See you around."

He felt a little sad when he walked down the stairs. Gino was a nice guy, but he couldn't lead him on. He had no intention of sticking around here if he didn't find Bruce.

He walked up Ste. Catherine again, checking every side

street looking for where he'd left his car. He stopped into a convenience store and bought a fifteen-dollar card for his phone.

He found his car, still intact, and got in, plugging the code into his cell phone. He pressed the message. *You have one message.* He pressed 1. "Hello, beautiful, it's Stephen Lachance. If you want Clay, he's here. Karl expects me to give him a job again. I just want to get rid of him. Bar opens at seven tonight. See you later."

August squeezed the phone in his hands. He let his head go back against the seat and closed his eyes. *I've found you. Finally, God damn it, I've found you.*

"Stephen is okay now with me being here?" Bruce sat with Karl in the kitchen at the bar and picked at his pasta.

"I don't know. He didn't say much. I'm sure he'll be fine. I didn't end up on the sofa."

"That's nice."

"Is something wrong with your pasta?"

"No. I don't have much of an appetite."

"Maybe it's the gin."

Bruce looked up in surprise.

"I saw you. I thought you were going to try."

"I can't sleep. I thought it might help."

"Clay? What is it you're running from? Is it the police?"

"No. Really, honest Karl. I didn't do anything."

"What is it then?"

"Shadows."

"What?"

He put down his fork and sighed. "It's just something in the past that doesn't exist. I'll try not to drink. Look, you got a doctor that could write me a prescription for something to calm my nerves?"

"Maybe. I can talk to him. I'm not sure. He's not much of

a pill doctor. How did you get the others, the ones you had when you came last time?"

"I met a guy who worked in a pharmacy."

"Aw."

"Karl, I won't stay long, just long enough to get some money together. I don't want to come between you and Stephen."

"It's okay."

"What's it like having someone in your life to care about you, love you, and wake up to?"

"Wonderful. Also, a pain sometimes," he grinned, "but I wouldn't have it any other way. Haven't you ever been in love, Clay?"

"No."

"That time we were . . ." he lowered his voice, "together, you weren't a virgin."

"No. I've had sex, sometimes it's just because I needed something, a ride, or some place to crash. Not with you that time." He smiled. "It was nice."

Karl nodded. "It was me getting back at Stephen."

"I know. But I liked it. I wanted to be close to someone, and you were nice to me."

"It's easy to be nice to you, kid."

"Don't," he put up a hand, "please don't call me kid, okay?"

"I'm sorry."

He shook his head. "Just this thing I have. Where's your better half anyway?"

"He's gone shopping to get some supplies."

"Oh. Let me help you clean up, okay? I'll pay you back for the gin."

They did the dishes together side by side in the little sink behind the bar, each lost in his own thoughts.

Bruce had the feeling that given the least little bit of encouragement, Karl would have let him fuck him; maybe just for old time's sake, or because Karl had always seemed to have a problem staying faithful. He was tempted, but not enough to jeopardize his place here.

Finally, just when they were getting ready to open, Stephen returned. "Hey, babe," he said, kissing Karl on the cheek. He nodded at Bruce.

Bruce nodded back and then swallowed his pride and walked up to him. "I want to work this time, Stephen. I promise not to mess up. I'll wait tables, dance. Remember how I used to bring in the crowd?"

He nodded. "Yes, I do. It's okay. Karl wants you here, so go ahead, find something to wear, and go to work."

"Tonight, I will work free and this weekend is free, okay?"

"Sure," Stephen replied and walked off to talk to the disc jockey. Karl squeezed his bicep. "He'll be all right."

"Good. "I'll go get ready."

August's stomach was in knots as he climbed the stairs. "We're not open yet," the man at the bar called out as August walked in.

"It's okay," Stephen said as he came to greet him. "I know this guy. Hello."

August shook his hand. "I appreciate this."

"No problem. He's here."

"Who's here?" The other man walked over now, wiping his hands on a towel. "Who is this?"

"My name is August Greystone."

"It's okay, Karl. He came here yesterday looking for Clay. I said that I'd call him if I saw him."

"Are you a policeman?" The one called Karl looked royally pissed off.

"No, not anymore. I just want to talk to him."

"You had no right," Karl snapped at Stephen.

"We'll talk about this later," Stephen muttered. "Come on, August. I'll take you to him."

"What do you think?" Bruce twirled around, showing off his sequined jock strap. He stopped when he saw Stephen and then a taller man with shoulder-length black hair standing behind him. "It's pretty flashy," he muttered, feeling embarrassed. "I thought you were Karl."

"No doubt," Stephen said. "Anyway," he turned to the other man, "here he is. I'll leave you to talk."

The other man turned his gaze to Bruce. Blue eyes, dark blue, the color of midnight, were examining him. There was something familiar about him, but he couldn't put his finger on it.

"Hello, Bruce," the man said.

Bruce's eyes widened. He backed up, knocked over the chair, and pressed his back against the clothes hanging off the coat rack. "Who are you? What do you want?"

"I'm not here to hurt you. I just want to . . ." He reached out.

Bruce cowered back in the corner. "Who in fuck are you? Leave me alone. I don't know you. I don't know anything, so go away."

The man lowered his hand. "Bruce, my name is August. I'm Tommy's brother. I've been trying to find you for so long, to talk to you. Please, let me —"

"No! No, leave me alone." He lunged at the man, pushed him out of the way, and ran out of the dressing room. In the bar, he looked around frantically. Where could he go? He wasn't even dressed. Where could he go? The room began to spin. A hand reached out for him, those blue eyes penetrated his gaze, and suddenly everything faded, everything went black, and he fell forward.

August stood there uncertainly with a half-naked, unconscious man in his arms. Karl raced to his side, and along with Stephen, they carried Bruce into the back room. Karl sat him in a chair, and Stephen brought a cold cloth while August stood in the corner, not sure what in hell just happened.

He studied the young man who had been his brother's summer friend. Although some years had passed and Bruce had grown taller and filled out some, he still looked like some kind of innocent blond angel.

"He's coming to," Karl said, looking into Bruce's face. "Clay, Clay, are you alright, honey? Talk to me."

"I'm, ah . . . what happened?" he asked, looking around. When his gaze settled on August, his expression hardened. "I don't know that man. I want him out of here." Karl turned around now. "You should go. You've upset him enough. You're what he's been running from, aren't you?" Karl turned back to Bruce. "Did he break your heart, honey?"

August scowled. "I'm not his fucking stalker boyfriend. Listen, God damn it, I just want to talk to him. I've been trying to find him for such a long time. Have some compassion, okay?" His voice broke.

August cleared his throat. "I need some air." He stumbled blindly through the bar and down the stairs. He stood outside for a moment. It was cold, but it was just what he needed to remind himself that he was still alive. He was unprepared for what seeing Bruce would do to him. And if Bruce refused to talk to him . . . *You're all I have . . . please.*

When the door opened ten minutes or so later, and Bruce came outside to join him, August didn't say anything.

Bruce leaned against the wall, and they stood side by side. He lit two cigarettes and handed him one. Bruce didn't ask him if he smoked.

"I'm sorry. I reacted badly," Bruce said.

August puffed on the cigarette, and then remembered how much he hated the filthy things. He crushed it beneath his foot and turned his head to look at Bruce. In fact, he couldn't stop looking at him. He hadn't changed much. He was still what one might call a pretty boy; his hair the same honey-blond that it was in that picture, but longer and straggly. He was slim, a little underweight really, and August estimated him to be about five ten or eleven, his head equal to August's shoulder. Bruce's hand shook as he put the cigarette to his lips. He was shivering from the cold.

"You should have a coat."

"Yeah," he laughed harshly, "I should have a lot of things." Bruce turned to him, his hazel green eyes sad and frightened. "I can't help you, August."

It was strange to hear his name from those lips. He wasn't sure if he hated or pitied him. He just knew that suddenly he wanted to reach out and shake him, but he wouldn't. The guy was severely fucked up, more fucked up than he thought he would be.

"I just wanted to talk."

"About what?" he demanded. "About the night Tommy died, about what happened that night?" His eyes were crazed suddenly. "What do you think I can tell you? You don't want to fucking know, okay?"

"Calm down," August told him. "Please. I didn't come here to upset you."

"Too late. Go away." Tears streamed down his face. "Please, leave me in peace."

"But you're not in peace, are you?"

He swallowed hard. "I pray every day for the nightmares to go away, for me not to hear his voice asking those fucking questions that I couldn't fucking answer. So, if you don't have any heavy drugs that will do that for me, get the fuck out of my sight." He threw the cigarette down and turned to go back inside.

"Wait," August reached out and grabbed his arm. "Please. Did you see him? Did you see his face? Could you have told the police anything that would have—"

"I see his eyes, cold and glassy, evil. Pure evil. I see them in my dreams." Bruce pulled his arm away and disappeared inside

August stayed in the same place for a long time and then took a long walk. He wasn't sure what to do now. Maybe all this time he'd spent tracking Bruce down had been in vain, a mistake. No, he couldn't let himself believe that. He'd given up everything. He took a deep breath and went to get coffee at a nearby shop. He knew he should eat, but he had no stomach for it.

He drank his coffee quickly and headed back to the bar.

Karl tried to comfort him, but Bruce knew he didn't understand. "Who is he, Clay? Why did he call you Bruce?"

"It's my real name," Bruce said, pacing the dressing room. He lit a cigarette, ignoring the no smoking sign on the wall.

"You knew him from before? He said he wasn't your lover."

"He wasn't my lover. This is the first time we've met."

"Then how does he know you?"

Bruce went over and looked out the window. He searched the street below. *Did he leave?*

"Clay? How does he know you?"

"I knew his brother."

"He looked upset."

"He is upset. He thinks I can do something for him, but I can't. I can't make it go away." He turned to look at Karl. "God, if I could just . . . I can't help him, damn it, I can't even help myself. I have no words to bring him comfort. If anything," he laughed harshly, "the contrary is true."

Suddenly, a voice asked, "What do you mean the contrary is true?" August Greystone stood in the doorway.

Karl glanced at him. "Clay, if you want me to . . ."

"It's okay, Karl," Bruce said, "you can leave us. He's not going to go away, and Stephen needs you in the bar. I'll be fine. I'll be ready for my dance set." The music was thumping now out in the bar. Some old disco queen declared "I love the nightlife, I got to boogie . . ." and Tommy's brother closed the door as Karl left.

"We'll be interrupted by the dancers soon. They change in here."

"Can we go somewhere later to talk?"

"We could, but then I already told you there's nothing to talk about."

"What did you mean when you said you had no words to comfort me? Do you think I came here for comfort?"

"No. You came here for closure, but I can't give you that either. You won't make me relive that night, no one will, even if you look so much like Tommy it fuckin' hurts." He lowered his voice. "I was half in love with him you know, an adolescent crush. He didn't know. He was oblivious, going on about pussy all the time." He looked at August. "He would have been a gorgeous man like you, if . . . Well, he might have looked like you."

August waited.

"Even though we would have never been lovers, we would have always been friends. We hit it off straight away when we met that summer. He was kind of goofy, more daring than I was, funny. He made me laugh. He loved you. He talked about you all the time. My brother, the cop, he'd say. He was obsessed with cops. Drove me a little crazy renting all those police movies."

"I was supposed to come home for his birthday," August said suddenly.

"Yeah," Bruce nodded, "I know."

August lowered his head. "Maybe if I'd come home I could have—"

"Could have what?" Bruce asked sharply. "Saved him? Nothing could have saved him."

"But he was around," August's voice was bitter, "lurking in those woods. He took your picture that day, this picture." August took out his wallet.

"I know the one." Bruce held up his hand. "I don't want to see it."

"He took it, didn't he? Didn't he?" August shoved the picture at him.

It fell to the floor.

Bruce turned his back.

August dragged him around to face him. "You must have seen him, spoken to him that day at Blood Pond. What did he look like? What was his name? Was he old, or young or—"

Bruce struggled out of his hold. "Stop it. I don't know. I don't remember, okay?"

"Clay," a voice said suddenly. "Is everything okay?" August took a step back.

Danny, one of the dancers, stood in the room. He looked at August curiously.

August looked down at the floor.

Bruce ran a hand through his hair. "I'm fine, really."

"You're on in five." The young dancer was still looking at August.

"I have to get dressed now, or undressed," Bruce announced with a snort.

"I'll go," August said as he turned and left the room.

"Who's the hunk?" Danny inquired.

"No one." Bruce looked at the open door. "He's no one."

"He's not yours then?"

"No. He's not mine."

Danny grinned. "So, it's open season?"

"No. Leave him alone." Bruce began to take off his clothes. "He's not your type."

August took a seat at the bar and motioned to Stephen. He walked over and put a glass in front of him.

"You look like shit. What are you drinking?"

"Whiskey, straight up. Make it a double." He took a bill out of his wallet and pushed it across the bar.

"Did you get what you came for?"

"No. Maybe what I've come for doesn't exist," he said as he watched Stephen pour the liquor.

"What's Clay's story?" Stephen asked. "He's obviously disturbed. He drinks too much, pops pills, everything stresses him out. Last year, remember I told you, he went nuts, smashed up the bar, and caused a shitload of damage? I have no idea what set him off."

August picked up the glass and swallowed some of the golden liquid. He coughed a little. It burned all the way down. The disc jockey put on some old Elvis tune, something about putting a chain around someone's neck, and August realized that Stephen was waiting for an answer.

"He's living in the past I guess."

"And you, handsome? Where are you living? It seems to me that you're living there with him."

August took another swallow, tasting it in his mouth. "I'm trying to find the man who murdered my brother."

"I'm sorry, man. I know Clay is a little wild, but he doesn't seem like the kind to —"

"No. He didn't kill my brother." August drained his glass and then put it back down on the bar. He turned around suddenly as he heard the disc jockey call out, "Welcome . . . the beautiful Clay!"

Some love song sung by a singer whose name escaped him poured out of the speakers as the men at the tables started to whistle and holler.

Bruce began to dance on the stage by himself, his eyes closed, moving his half-naked body to ... *hold me in your arms and love me tonight* ... The crowd was riveted. Bruce's hands moved over his own chest and snaked inside the jock he wore, and suddenly August couldn't tear himself away. *We shouldn't be ... forbidden passions in the deep night ... but your touch so ignites me ... so enraptured by your eyes ... love me tonight ... love me ... and forget the morning light ... forget that you don't belong to me ... can't belong to me ...*

One side of the jock strap now hung loose, his thigh exposed, the material dangerously close to slipping down and leaving him completely naked. He moved his hips, humping the steel post that was at center stage, and slid his finger down to unhook the other side of the strap. His eyes were still closed. He was lost in his own thoughts.

There was nothing left to the imagination now as his smooth, round ass flashed around the pole and he took the strap in his hand and flipped it up in the air. Several men in the audience scrambled to get it, flushed, excited.

Twenty-dollar bills fluttered onto the stage, catcalls and wolf whistles abounded, and the applause was deafening as the song died down. Bruce lowered himself onto the floor of the stage, arms stretched out over his head, as he lifted his hips upwards in the air.

The music ended. The disc jockey called out his name again, speaking rapidly in French, and it was over. Bruce collected his money off the stage and disappeared into a room in the back.

"That's why I let him stay," Stephen said suddenly as August turned back to the bar, a little stunned. It was as if he were two different men; the one on stage bold and seductive, the other withdrawn and jittery. "He brings in the crowd,"

Stephen announced, "but he's one fucked-up piece of work. You want another drink?"

"No." He stood up. He couldn't afford another drink. He looked toward the back room.

The one called Karl came over to him suddenly. He put up a hand. "Where are you going?"

August looked down at him. "I wasn't going to go anywhere."

"Leave Clay alone."

"His name is Bruce, and this isn't any of your business."

"No, but this is my bar. I'd like you to leave."

"Karl," Stephen came around to join them, "there's no need to be rude."

August shook his head. "It's all right. I'm going." He looked at Karl. "Can you give him my phone number? Can you ask him, please, to call me? I'll wait around for a few days."

Stephen nodded. "I have your number. I'll give it to him."

August looked at Karl. "I know you don't understand. I know you think that maybe I'm harassing him in some way, but I think he needs me as much as I need him. He's suffering much more than I imagined. If he'd just talk to me . . ." August broke off.

Karl nodded. "I'll see what I can do. Okay?"

August thanked him, thanked them both, and headed for the exit. Suddenly, as he got to the stairs, a hand snaked out. He turned around in anticipation, thinking maybe it was Bruce and he'd changed his mind.

It was one of the dancers. "I'm Danny. Do you remember? We met in the dressing room."

"Yeah, I remember."

"Where you going?"

"I don't know," he said. "Not sure."

"Place closes at three. If you wait around, we could get a

drink?"

August considered the invitation. It would be a way to stay close by, maybe get Bruce to change his mind, but he decided to pass. If Bruce wouldn't talk to him, he couldn't force him. He wasn't sure whatever made him think Bruce would talk to him.

"Sweetheart?" the guy said. "Is that a yes?"

August shook his head. "Sorry. I'm a little tired. Thanks anyway." He started down the stairs.

"Are you coming back tomorrow night?" he called out down the stairs.

August walked out without giving him an answer.

It was colder tonight, and the air was damp. He could have sworn he saw tiny flakes of white in the air. He walked quickly, wishing he could just end this, go home, and have a normal life like everyone else. But how? How could he finish this? How was it supposed to end? Was Bruce supposed to give him the exact description of a serial killer he'd seen over ten years ago? Then what? Would he go on a quest to find him? Was he still alive? Was he around the corner? Was he living in Amsterdam? Or was he where August suspected he was, back at Blood Pond?

Hey, Bro, when you coming home? When you coming home? When you coming home?

He walked faster. The cold air filled his lungs. He smashed into a guy on the corner and kept walking, ignoring the cursing in French that wafted after him. He finally stopped, out of breath. He found a bench and sat down as the traffic whizzed by. Two young men walked by with a black lab, and a homeless man asked him for change. He only gave him a quarter because he was almost as bad off as the homeless man.

Come home, August. This won't bring Tommy back. We've lost him. I don't want to lose you too. Can't we just put it behind us?
His mother had been all alone after Tommy was murdered.

His father had died when August was ten, and late last year, his mother had died, too, of a sudden heart attack.

But could he put it behind him?

I'm sorry, August, we couldn't do it. The coffin will have to be closed. We did the best we could to put . . . what was left . . . of him together but . . .

"God," he whispered to no one, putting his face in his hands. The tears flooded his eyes. It had been a long time since he'd had any tears to cry. He looked up, and suddenly, the sky opened and cried with him, the cold rain running down his face, mingling in sympathy with his tears.

Several people squealed as they came out of various buildings, running along the sidewalk to find sanctuary. He ran a hand through his wet hair, and somewhere a phone rang, and finally realized it was his. He dug it out of his wet pants pocket and flipped it open. "Hello?"

"August?" the voice said.

"Bruce?"

"Come back. I'm ready to talk."

He closed his eyes and flipped his phone closed.

CHAPTER FOUR

Bruce's eyes widened a little when he opened the door to his room upstairs and saw August standing there, dripping all over the floor. "I guess it's raining outside."

"You guess?"

He had told Karl and Stephen to send August right upstairs when he came in. He just hadn't expected him to resemble a drowned rat. He looked kind of funny; his long black hair hanging in strands around his face, his jeans sagging because they were so heavy with water. "Take off your jacket. I'll get you a towel. You can dry off."

"I may never be dry again," August grumbled.

Bruce ran off to find a towel and came back with two big ones. "Here."

He watched as August shrugged out of his leather jacket. He took it from him and hung it over the chair.

"Thanks," August said.

"You might want to take off your t-shirt."

August pulled it over his head.

Bruce tried hard not to notice the muscles that ran across his chest and waved over his abdominals. He was wet and hard, totally all man.

August rubbed the towel over his biceps and his chest. It wasn't meant to be erotic, but in the intimacy of the small room, it felt like that to Bruce, and there was no reason that it should have. It was a distraction, and maybe he needed that right now. He was going to suggest that August take off his jeans too, but he knew it would sound like a come-on.

"You can sit down," Bruce said.

There were two chairs in the corner by a little table.

"The heat is on. It's warm by the register."

August sat, his dark hair hanging in disarray around his face. He had at least two days' growth of beard on his face. It made him look dangerous but in a very sensual way. "Are you living in your car?" Bruce needed to focus on something else for a minute. Desire was not a feeling that came to him often, but right now he felt possessed by it. He could even taste it in his mouth.

"More or less."

Bruce sat across from him, his body stiff as if he were waiting for an attack. There was only a small light burning in the corner. A neon sign flashed off and on across the street. Downstairs, the music played from the jukebox, some Frank Sinatra tune from the Rat Pack days. It was almost closing time. "How do you live, eat?"

"I do private investigations. Sometimes I can do that through the internet, or I just stay in one place for enough time to finish the job."

"What about your job on the police force?" He just shrugged. "I don't understand. You've lived this way just so you could find me?"

"Yes." Their eyes met.

"You've done it for nothing."

"So you said."

"What do you think I can tell you, August? I can't change anything." He was shaking again.

August reached over and captured his hand. "You're afraid."

"Yes, I'm afraid." He jerked his hand away like he'd just been burned and jumped up from his seat. "In fact, I'm fucking terrified every minute of every day. And now, at night, it's worse, and being here with you, talking about this . . ."

"Not talking about it won't change anything."

"I know that." He dropped back into the chair "That's why I called you. If it helps you, if somehow what I have to say saves you, then I'm willing to talk."

"You'll do it to save me?" He laughed a little. "You don't even know me. Why would you want to save me?"

His eyes filled with tears. "Because I couldn't save him."

"It wasn't your fault." August grabbed his hand again. "It wasn't your job to save Tommy. How did you survive? Just tell me that much. Tell me how you got away from him."

Bruce didn't remove his hand for a moment.

August released it finally and sat back.

Bruce got back up and stood by the window. He watched the sign blink on and off. The young man, handsome and fit, leered at the onlookers, naked except for a pair of skin-tight jeans. Off and on, off and on . . . He gripped the sill. One night, the light would go out and stay out.

Suddenly, he felt August behind him. He sucked in his breath, turned, and looked into August's blue eyes. "I watched your brother die."

August swallowed hard. How could anyone ever be the same after that? How do you not close your eyes and not see it, watch it play over and over again?

Bruce . . . don't.

Shut up.

"Help me find him, Bruce. Make him pay."

"How can you find someone who doesn't exist? How do you find a shadow?"

"But he does exist."

Bruce shook his head. "No. As long as he doesn't find me, he doesn't exist."

"Is that what you tell yourself? Is that how you make it all right?" August's voice rose an octave. "That's fine for you, you're alive. My brother is dead. It wasn't a nightmare. It wasn't some sort of ghost who killed my brother. It was a

50

man, a real man."

"And I wish it was me!" Bruce hollered. "I wish it was me who was dead. God," he started to cry, "I wish it was me he'd killed."

August's arms wrapped around him, and he struggled. He didn't want comfort. He didn't deserve comfort. August held tight until he collapsed against him.

August wasn't sure what to do. He just kept holding onto him as agonizing sobs wracked Bruce's body, seeming to come from the depths of his very soul. August closed his eyes, absorbed his pain, and reconnected with his own as Bruce's arms wound tighter around his waist. After a while, he quieted, but he still held onto him as if August were a life raft out in the middle of the ocean.

"I'm sorry," Bruce told him. He stood back, his face streaked with tears. "I need a drink."

August watched as Bruce went to the bed and took a half-empty bottle out from under it. "Want some?" he asked.

He shook his head. "No. I'm really tired, and if I drink, I'll pass out."

"You can stay here tonight if you want." He looked at him.

August looked at the bed. "I don't think so."

"I won't molest you," Bruce scoffed and tipped the bottle to his lips, "although some rough, raunchy sex wouldn't be such a bad thing, especially with a man who looks as good as you do. But then, I'd remember who you are."

"That's not what I . . . I mean . . ."

"I'm gay. Guess you got that."

"Yeah. I got that." He didn't think it productive to tell Bruce that he was, too. It didn't matter. He hadn't come here for that.

"I wouldn't be much good in bed anyway," Bruce said,

sitting on the edge of the bed. "Come to think of it, aside from a few blow jobs and getting screwed up the ass a few times in payment for something or other, I'm somewhat virginal." He laughed at that.

"I'm sorry." He'd had his share of lovers before Tommy died, but after . . . Well, he'd tried to work, tried to go back to policing, even had a lover, but it was hard. Nothing made much sense after Tommy. *You're emotionally void . . . you can't feel anything . . . you're always depressed . . . you should see someone . . . you should . . .*

"I didn't see him, you know."

"Huh?"

"Him, I didn't see him." Bruce had drunk down quite a bit of the liquor in the bottle which relaxed him. The tension was gone from his shoulders. He wiped his mouth with the back of his hand. The club was quiet downstairs now. There were voices below in the street.

"Not even that day at Blood Pond?"

"No. It was Tommy who went to get the picture. He was standing in the trees. I saw his arm. I remember it was muscular, tanned, with dark, downy hair."

"You never saw his face at all?"

"He wore a mask the entire time."

"Was he tall, short, fat?"

"Tall I think, but he seemed like a giant to me." He looked at August now, his eyes dry, voice steady.

"Did he have an accent? What was his voice like?"

"No accent. He sounded like every other man, voice was deep, smooth. He had a light, airy laugh, like a . . . a . . . young boy. Funny. He had a voice like a man, but he laughed like a boy."

"You were there with him for twelve hours, thirteen?"

He shook his head. "Less, it was early evening when . . ." he took another drink, "when he took us to that place, seven or eight maybe. It wasn't yet light when I was running through the woods. I remember because I couldn't see. I bumped into a few trees, went around and round while he . . . he . . . called my name, laughed at me. He was sure, so sure that he'd catch me."

"But he didn't."

"No," he shook his head, "and yet I've never been free of him." Bruce stood, tipped over his empty bottle. "All gone."

"Where did you hide?"

"In Blood Pond. It was an accident. I ran right into it, and it saved my life. I dove under the water, and I stayed there. I thought my lungs would burst. And then I heard this movement, heard the low sound of a motor on a boat. It was Mr. Simpson. He always went fishing just before dawn. Do you remember him? He lived just down from your summer house."

August nodded. "Yes. He died a few years back."

"When I heard him, I brought my head up and took a breath. I figured that Simpson had scared him off. I was right."

"Didn't Mr. Simpson see you?"

"No. I waited until he got into the middle of the lake then I scrambled up out of the pond. By that time, it was light. I walked along the road. I'm not sure how long or how far I walked. I don't think I knew who I was for days. I just kind of blanked out."

"And no one tried to help you or —"

"Every time I saw anyone, I ran. I hid. And eventually, it all came back, everything. I remember hearing people talking about it, and you know, I couldn't even connect to it. Then I saw Tommy's picture one time on a television playing in a store window in Newport, Vermont, and I smashed the window. The owner made me work it off, and I stayed there awhile. After that, I just went from town to town, picking up work here and there. You know, I was always afraid that he was still behind me, still chasing me through those woods."

August didn't say anything. There was nothing to say. They were both caught in the same headlights.

"What are you wasting your life for?" Bruce asked him. "Go back to Manchester; go back to the police force.

Live. You can't bring Tommy back. And do you really want to find this guy?"

"He murdered my brother, and he's out there, living his life and—"

Bruce shook his head. "I don't want to know who he is."

"How can you say that?"

"Because you weren't there. You didn't watch him hack your brother into . . . You didn't have to watch him die."

"Doesn't that make you want to see him pay?"

"No! I just want him to stay away from me."

"You're a coward. Goddamn it, Bruce, you're a fucking coward. You are so afraid, you're paralyzed. You were his friend. Don't you care?"

"Fuck you. Just fuck you," Bruce muttered and headed for the door. "I need a drink."

August reached out and grabbed him. "You don't need anything else to drink, Goddamnit. You need closure. You need to be able to sleep at night, knowing that he can't hurt you anymore. You need to help me."

Bruce tried to pull away, but August held him fast.

"Let me go."

"No. Now that I've found you, I'll never let you go, Bruce, until we catch this monster. And you're the only one who can help me do it. Please. Please, come with me."

"Come with you where?"

"New Hampshire. Back to the summer house."

A cold chill ran up Bruce's spine. "No, August, no."

"Bruce, listen to me. About two months ago, he . . ."

Bruce stared at him. He could scarcely breathe.

"What happened two months ago?"

"A fifteen-year-old boy went missing. His body was discovered within thirty miles of that old abandoned shack where you and Tommy were taken. He'd been hacked to pieces with a machete. They found the head in Blood Pond."

"Jesus Christ," Bruce moaned. He ceased to struggle as the neon sign went out and they were both left standing in the dark.

August was the first to move. He walked over and switched on the lamp on the nightstand beside the old cast iron double bed. August looked at it with longing, realizing suddenly that he was exhausted. "We'll get started in the morning."

"I didn't say I was coming."

"Bruce. Please." August turned to him. "I think he came back for you this time. The boy was around the same age as you were and blond."

"Don't fucking say that."

"He came back to finish what he started. It didn't matter that it wasn't you. You're probably the only one who ever got away."

Bruce visibly swallowed.

"He'll kill again." When Bruce didn't comment, August added, "He's still there."

"You don't know that."

"I just feel it."

Bruce met his gaze.

"I won't let anything happen to you. I promise."

"Don't make promises you can't keep." Bruce walked to the door and opened it. "You can't stay in your car, and you should get those wet clothes off. I'll see if Karl has any sweat pants or . . ." Bruce was rambling, but August understood why.

"I have clothes in my car."

"You'll catch your death going out like that. I'm sure he won't mind. We can hang yours in the bathroom to dry."

August nodded. There was no point arguing about this. His feet were soaked, and his wet pants still clung to his chilled legs. Suddenly, he was alone. He walked over to the window and looked down into the alley. He closed his eyes for a moment, letting the weariness drag over him. He glanced longingly over his shoulder at the bed. Maybe he could just lay his head on the pillow for a minute.

Karl and Stephen were still cleaning up. "Need a hand?" Bruce asked.

"We're almost through," Karl said. "How's it going with, ah . . ."

Bruce shrugged. "It's okay. Look, he's pretty wet. I wonder if you'd have a pair of sweats or something to lend him just until his clothes dry."

"Sure. I'll go upstairs and get him some. He'll need a t-shirt and socks, too, I imagine."

"Thanks, Karl."

Karl threw down his towel and disappeared.

Bruce stood around uncomfortably, not sure what to say to Stephen. Stephen came over and fixed him with his gaze. "I know you've been drinking again. I didn't tell Karl. I want you out of here."

"I'm leaving tomorrow."

"Good, you'll be his problem."

"Stephen. I'm sorry for the problems I've caused you. You and Karl have been kind to me and—"

"Look, Bruce, I don't wish you any ill will. I just hope whatever is eating you, well, you find a way to live with it."

"It's good advice. I'm going to try. It won't be easy."

"It might have helped if you'd have confided in us."

"Stephen," Bruce said, reaching out and clutching his forearm, "I could barely stand to confess it to myself.

Maybe one day it will get easier to talk about."

Stephen nodded. "Good luck."

A few minutes later, Karl came down with a care package. He handed it to Bruce, sweat pants, socks, t-shirt, towels. "Hope that helps."

"Perfect. We'll be leaving in the morning."

"Are you sure? You can stay, you know. It's not Stephen who's making you go, is it?"

"No. It's time," he said.

They said goodnight. Karl hugged him. "Take care, honey," he whispered.

Bruce kissed him on the forehead. "You, too."

"Will you come back?"

"I'll try."

Karl walked him to the bottom of the stairs.

Bruce was thinking about Karl as he walked into the room, how kind he'd been to him, how they'd come to care about each other in such a short time. When he walked into the room and closed the door, he spotted August lying on the bed. As he drew closer, he noticed that the man was sound asleep. He put the things down on the table and sighed. He studied him for a minute. He hated to wake him, but he couldn't let him sleep in wet pants like that. "August," he said, shaking him a little, "wake up. You have to take off those pants."

"Hmm?" His eyes opened, and he looked at him sleepily.

Bruce couldn't help but smile. He was so handsome; a sweet, dopey smile on his lips.

"Sorry," he yawned, sitting up, "I fell asleep."

"You got the bed all wet," Bruce said.

"No," he protested. He got up. "My jacket was dry. I slept

on that."

"Get those clothes off. You can take a hot shower in the bathroom. I guess we can share the bed," he said hesitantly.

"You have nothing to worry about from me," he muttered. "I'm too damn tired to do anything about it."

Bruce met his gaze. "You're gay then?"

"Does it make a difference? If I say yes, will I have to sleep on the floor?"

He laughed a little. "No. Just seems strange, that's all."

"What seems strange?"

"You being gay."

"I didn't say I *was* gay."

"Well, if you were, I mean . . . if we'd met before, maybe . . . I had a big crush on you."

"Correction. You had a big crush on Tommy."

"Yeah, but I saw your picture and . . . never mind. You were too old for me."

He laughed. "Yeah. Too old. Where's the bathroom?"

"That door beside the closet." Bruce indicated which door with a toss of his head. "Take your time. I'm going to bed."

The door closed, and a few minutes later, he heard the shower running. Bruce stripped off his clothes down to the underwear and quickly crawled under the covers. The bed was a little damp where August had lain, but it was okay. He closed his eyes, the sound of the running water easing him into sleep.

Don't you want him, Bruce? Don't you want him to fuck you?

He was vaguely aware of someone slipping into bed beside him. He turned onto his side, snuggled down into the pillow and slept.

When he opened his eyes, the sun was shining through the window. He put his hand up in front of his face and then turned to see that he was alone. He sat up and stretched. For the first time in a long time, he felt rested. He'd actually slept through the night without having one single nightmare.

He got up to use the bathroom. August's wet clothes were gone, so were the sweatpants that Karl had lent him. Maybe he'd changed his mind and decided to leave without him. He took a quick shower, changed his clothes and put his belongings in his knapsack. When he went downstairs, he found August sitting at the bar drinking coffee and talking with Karl and Stephen.

"Everyone is up early," he announced.

"Honey," Karl said, "it's after eleven. Coffee?"

After eleven? Holy shit! "Yeah, okay." He looked at August. "Sorry to hold you up."

"No problem. I had some stuff to do."

"You want breakfast?" Stephen asked him.

"Just toast."

"Can do," he replied and went into the back kitchen to make some.

August's car was a rather battered looking Toyota. He threw his knapsack into the back seat and crawled into the front. As they drove out of the city, Bruce wondered what in hell he was doing. Why had he agreed to go back to New Hampshire with him?

"Did you know him?" Bruce asked as they began to cross the bridge.

It was raining again. August switched on the windshield wipers. "Know who?"

"The boy they found in Blood Pond?"

"No."

"Where are we going to stay?"

"At the summer house."

Bruce wrapped his arms around himself. "Will your mother mind?"

"My mother's dead."

"Oh, I didn't know. When did she die?"

"Last year, heart attack."

"She wasn't old."

"No."

"Tommy told me he didn't remember your father. He died young too."

"Yes, he did. He worked in construction. Someone forgot to check that the scaffold was secure, and he fell."

"Damn."

"I remember my father, but Tommy was not even five years old."

"So, you don't have any children or . . ."

"Bruce," he glanced at him, "just ask, okay?"

"Are you?"

"Yes."

"I thought so."

"Really?"

"It's just that you seemed comfortable in that gay bar. And you didn't take your eyes off me once when I was dancing."

August kept his eyes on the road.

"Come on," Bruce said, "'fess up."

He laughed. "If you say so."

"I say so." Bruce paused. "So, as Danny said, you're open season."

"Danny? Oh, the dancer. He said I was open season?" August asked.

"Something like that. Did he hit on you?"

"Ah . . . I wouldn't call it hitting on me. Well, maybe."

Bruce laughed faintly. "Where I come from, you either get hit on, or you don't. You're the kind who gets hit on."

"Is that a compliment?"

"No. It's a fact. Can I ask a stupid question?"

"Sure."

"Do we have enough gas in this thing to get back to New Hampshire?"

"Nope."

"Great."

"It's okay," August said. "I wrote Stephen a check for next week, and he gave me some cash."

"Is it going to bounce?"

"No, it's not going to bounce."

"Good. You're lucky. Stephen doesn't like me much."

"Could it be because last time you were in his place, you smashed it up?"

"That could be it."

August glanced at him. He laughed a little. They crossed the bridge, and August drove for a while. He found the exit for Granby and headed to the Eastern Townships.

"We should be there by suppertime," Bruce said.

"How long has it been since you saw your mother?"

"A while."

"You don't call her?" August asked.

"No."

"Does she know?"

"That I was with him? No, I think she believes I'm just traumatized by Tommy's murder overall. I think she'd freak if I told her the truth."

"She didn't even report you missing when you left. You're not close."

"No."

"Maybe if you confided in her . . ."

"You said it yourself, we're not close."

"I think you should have talked to someone."

"Why?"

"So that you don't live through this alone."

"Like you?" Bruce asked.

August didn't reply. After a few minutes, he said, "I never thought you'd come with me."

"Me neither, and I still might jump out of this car at any time."

"Hmm. I guess we won't stop to pee then."

Bruce settled back in the seat. He smiled. "Tommy had your sense of humor, dry, a little sarcastic. Or he could be a clown. Your mom would get so peeved at him."

"I know."

"Can we stop to pee soon? I have to go."

"Ha, ha."

"No, I'm not kidding."

August sighed.

"Plus, I'm starving. The least you could do is feed me. Did Stephen give you enough to spring for a hamburger?"

"Yeah, he did." August nodded. "The next rest-stop I see with a hamburger place, I'll pull off."

"Great. Hey," he reached into his pocket and took out a bill, "I found a five."

"Great. Buy your own hamburger then."

"The last of the great big spenders."

"I'm not trying to get you into bed."

Bruce's eyes widened. "For a hamburger?"

August glanced at him and grinned. "Yeah, because right now, kid, that's all I got, believe me."

Oh no. He has way more than that, doesn't he? He's hot . . . one big hunk. "You're a good-looking man. Under any other circumstances, I would have bought *you* a hamburger."

August gave him an odd look as he took the next exit.

Had he said that aloud?

"Do you often laugh to yourself?" August asked him when they got out of the car.

"You know what?" Bruce told him, "No. I don't. In fact, it's been a long time since I really found much to laugh about at all."

"Glad I amuse you," August said as he walked up to the

counter to order.

Bruce headed to the washroom.

They ate hamburgers and fries, drank icy Cokes, and then finally got back into the car. "If you get tired, I'll drive," Bruce offered.

"It's okay. Driving relaxes me."

So does fucking.

Another half hour and they were at the border. They showed their passports to the guard and went through Newport. It was then that Bruce started to panic.

August had seen people have anxiety attacks before. When he was on the police force, he'd seen plenty. Bruce's was especially acute. August pulled off on the side of the road and watched as Bruce paced up and down, struggling for breath, and then threw up. He kept telling August it would pass.

Eventually, it did, but he broke out into a cold sweat and seemed drained of energy. He looked so fragile, so broken sitting there in the passenger seat as they headed on toward Lancaster that August suddenly felt a surge of protectiveness toward him. That bastard. How many lives had he torn apart? All those innocent lives he'd taken, but the lives of those who had to live with the horror of it weren't counted. That night when he'd taken Tommy's life, he'd also taken August's, their mother's, Bruce's, and Bruce's mother had also lost her son that night.

He kept driving, but something prompted him to reach for Bruce's hand. He just wanted to keep him safe, and as they passed Mountain Lake Campgrounds and Mount Pleasant came into view, that feeling of wanting to keep him safe grew ever more intense.

As they drove off the road passed the Waumbek Golf Course, Bruce craned his neck. Not far from here was the

Black Brook Trail. How often he and Tommy had hiked there that summer. They'd gone kayaking over the rapids of Israel River, and Bruce had thought they were going to drown. It had been a lot of fun.

Blood Pond was close.

So am I.

So was the summer house that belonged to the Greystone family.

The car had already come to a standstill in front of the little stone cottage, and Bruce was still picturing that lake, Blood Pond, and its twin, Martin Meadow.

"Bruce?"

He blinked, then looked over at the big, tall, handsome dark-haired man sitting beside him.

"We're here."

The sun was going down now. It was going to be cold, probably down to twenty, maybe even ten degrees tonight.

As if reading his mind, August said as he got out of the car, "I have lots of warm clothes."

"Good." Bruce shivered, pulling his knapsack out of the back. He wasn't sure what he was doing here. It didn't make much sense coming back here. He hadn't been here since . . . It didn't matter anyway, did it?

Do you know I'm here?

Yes.

August took his arm and pulled him up the steps. He dug out his key and put it in the lock. "I haven't been here since late July. We might want to air it out."

It did smell a little musty, but it was just like Bruce remembered it, the green brocade sofas in the living room, the mocha carpets, and wood furniture, even down to those little hand-crocheted doilies on the coffee table.

"You can take my room," he said. "I'll take my mothers. It's a little frilly. I've been meaning to redecorate."

Bruce nodded. "First room on the left, right?"

64

"That's it," August called out. "I'm going out back to get some wood."

Bruce froze and told himself to relax. August wasn't far away. He flipped on the light in the room and put down his bag. He smiled as he looked at the walls; pictures of fancy sports cars, football heroes, and a couple of police cars. On the mirror hung a picture of August and Tommy, dressed in ski suits, arms around each other, probably the winter before Tommy died. He picked it up and studied it then put it back on the mirror.

He sunk down onto the bed and put his face in his hands. What did August want from him? It pained him to be here. Tommy's room was just down the hall.

He was at the door. "Find everything you need?"

"Sure. It's great."

"Good. What do you want to eat? I can do pasta and sauce. We'll have to get some food tomorrow."

"Pasta is fine. Where was that taken?" He pointed to the picture.

"Cannon Mountain. Ski trip."

"I always wanted to learn to ski."

"I'll teach you if you like."

"I won't be here that long," he said.

August nodded. "Supper will be ready in half an hour."

They didn't talk a lot during the meal. Bruce listened to the wind move the trees outside. The branches tapped incessantly against the dining room window as August poured fresh hot coffee into their cups. "How long do you think this is going to take?"

"I don't know."

"What are we doing exactly?"

"I need you to walk me through that night."

Bruce felt his stomach juices working a little. The bile rose in his throat. He swallowed some coffee. "That place, I'm not going there."

"The owner tore it down anyway, or it burned down, not sure. I don't go there either."

"Oh."

"Maybe the police missed something, something they wouldn't have missed if you'd told them you were there."

"How many times do I have to tell you, August? I didn't see his face. He wore a bizarre mask. Tommy saw him that day in the woods, but he—"

"Think. Did he say anything about him after he got the picture? Did he act like he knew him, like he'd seen him before?"

Bruce put the mug down and cleared his throat. "Do you have anything for acid reflux?"

"Maybe." August got up. "I'll check the medicine cabinet. Think."

He sighed, closed his eyes, and tried to picture that day.

It had been warm, almost no breeze. It was hot even in the shade. They'd been horsing around, in and out of water, and by suppertime, they were exhausted, famished.

"What do you want to eat?" Tommy asked him. His skin looked so tanned, his muscles smooth and taut. Bruce could see that the water had given Tommy a slight erection.

He tried not to look there. He had one, too.

"I don't know. Pizza?"

"I can ask Mom to order in." He flopped down on the beach towel. "Want to stay over?"

"Sure, but no police movies, okay? Let's rent a comedy."

"Okay."

Bruce had turned onto his stomach because by looking at Tommy lying there half-naked, his skin moist and his bathing trunks tented, he was getting a woody himself, and he didn't want Tommy to see. He didn't want him to know. They had too much fun together to ruin it. Tommy would run ten miles if he thought for a minute that Bruce was thinking about him that way. But he was.

He wanted to pull down those trunks and look at it, touch it, taste it. Suck it.

"You got quiet. What are you daydreaming about?" Tommy asked. "That little blonde with the big jugs we saw swimming yesterday?"

"Yeah," he said, "that's it."

Bruce didn't notice the figure standing in the bushes and neither did Tommy until he took the picture. Before he turned over to see what was happening, Tommy was talking to the man in the woods. Bruce saw that arm reach out and hand Tommy the picture. He remembered Tommy saying, "Gee thanks, man."

And then Tommy was down on the ground on the towel showing him that picture. "Pretty cool, eh?" he said with a laugh.

"Who was that guy?"

"This stuff is probably past its expiration date," August announced as he walked back into the dining room with a box of pills.

"He was camping at Roger's Campground," Bruce blurted out.

August stopped dead. "What?"

"The guy who took the picture. He was camping at Roger's. I remember now. I remember Tommy saying that."

August put the box on the table. "What else did he say?"

Bruce shook his head. "I don't know, just that. Maybe other stuff. I have to think."

"When was that photograph taken? How long was it between the time he took that photo and the night Tommy died?"

Bruce closed his eyes. He tried to push his memory back to those warm summer days, those days when nothing seemed to matter except the water and the sun and Tommy's laughter. Even all the fighting that went on in his house faded into the background when Tommy came by on his bicycle in the morning to get him. Sometimes he'd ride him on

Tommy's handlebars, and they'd slide and swerve all over the gravel roads on the way to the lake, laughing like two fools.

"He'd been depressed on his birthday," Bruce said. "He thought you were coming. He wanted me to meet you. He said you were really cool."

August nodded regretfully. He'd had a really hot date that weekend. He'd spent the weekend of his brother's birthday fucking.

"He had a little bit of a fight with your mother, not a fight really, a kind of an outburst. He took off for a walk on his own, and it was late. I went after him at your mother's insistence, and we talked down by the water. I remember thinking that someone was watching us that night. I felt as if we weren't alone. And I swear I heard something in the bushes. Tommy said it was just some dumb animal. He had that picture with him, so I know that it was taken before his birthday."

"Tommy's birthday was on July 2nd, and he died on July 17th. That's just over two weeks."

Bruce nodded. "I don't know how that helps anything."

"Campgrounds keep records of their guests." August snapped his fingers. "We could check who was staying there at that time. It gives us a starting place."

"That was a long time ago. You think they still have those records? And what if he lied to Tommy and he was a local?"

"I've considered that, but given the similarities of the murders that were all committed in different camping regions of New Hampshire, chances are he moves around."

"Like you and I?"

August smiled faintly. "Touché."

"Do you think he camps in each place, that there would be a record of the same guy in . . ."

August looked at him. "You sound as if you might be interested in helping me now."

"He'd be pretty stupid, wouldn't he?"

"Yeah. I doubt he registers at every local campground. But maybe, just maybe, he did stay at Roger's.

I know the people who used to run it. They're retired now. They might remember, might have kept a record."

"Do you really think that was him, the same one who just killed this local boy?"

"Yes. Unless it was a copycat, but I don't think so."

"I feel as if I've run the marathon," Bruce said.

"I think you know a lot of things, Bruce, but you've repressed them on purpose."

"I'm not going to a shrink."

"Okay, but let me play shrink with you a little bit, okay? I promise I won't pressure you to go any further than you want to."

Bruce grinned. "Sounds like I'm a virginal little girl out on the first date with an experienced older man."

"Well, you did say, aside from a few things that didn't count, that you were virginal." August smirked.

Bruce nodded. "So I did. And you're a flirt, Mr. Greystone."

August looked surprised. "Seriously, I think you're the flirt. Now, go to bed, and we'll talk more in the morning. I'll lock up.

Bruce wished him good night and went into August's old room. He sorely wanted to walk into Tommy's bedroom, but he fought the urge. He wasn't sure what that would feel like. Anyway, he had a feeling that many of the things he'd have to do in the coming days would be difficult, especially remembering things he'd much rather forget, but he'd made his decision. August was right. He couldn't keep running from shadows.

I watched him take his head, August.

CHAPTER FIVE

August found it difficult to sleep. He now associated being in this house for any length of time with painful changes. He remembered coming back here after Tommy had been murdered. They'd had the reception right out there in the living room. It had been very uncomfortable, very tense. No one knew what to say about the unsolved murder, the closed coffin, the severed head; it had been a shocking and unnatural event. The next time he came back here was to attend another funeral, his mother's, who had died unexpectedly. He surmised it was from grief. Finally, he'd given up his career to live in poverty in order to find Bruce, who may or may not be able to help him track down his brother's murderer in the end. There was no happiness in this house, and the only reason he hung onto it was because letting go would mean giving up. And he couldn't do that.

Right now, seriously, he wasn't sure what in hell he was doing anymore. It was a jumble in his head. The thought that the killer may have stalked Tommy and Bruce for almost two weeks before he'd kidnapped them, completely consumed him. That's why sleep wouldn't take him. His mind was filled with the possibilities. Just maybe that meant that people had seen the killer in town, talked with him, and they could remember something that might uncover his identity. If he had something tangible, the police might be persuaded to reopen the case. Maybe with this last murder, they already had made some connections. He needed to talk to Desmond.

He knew the family of this young boy who'd been murdered. He'd gone to school with Washington Jones' mother. They'd been in the same grade. Martha Jones had been pregnant right out of high school with Washington. August's mother had gone to the baby shower. When he closed his eyes, he could see Washington playing in Martha's back yard as a youngster.

Bruce startled him suddenly when he said his name. For a moment, he'd forgotten he wasn't alone in the house. He'd been alone so much; alone in his thoughts, alone in his life. No one wanted to share a life with someone obsessed with the past, with someone who fell into depression or stared off in the distance without provocation.

"Are you all right?"

August realized he was standing in the middle of the living room. How did he get here? He didn't even remember getting out of bed. "Yes. You?"

"I had a dream."

"Another nightmare?" August asked him.

"No." Bruce shook his head. "I dreamt that I was walking through the center of town and you were waiting for me. You seemed so far away. You kept telling me to come, but I . . . well, I woke up. I never arrived."

August clasped a hand on his shoulder. "You will arrive. Want coffee?"

"God, it's only eight o'clock. But yeah, I'm awake now."

They took their coffee on the front porch. It was going to be an unusually warm day for this time of year. The sun was bright, almost punishing. They stood leaning against the railing, coffee in hand. He looked at Bruce.

God, Bruce was young, good-looking. He had his entire life ahead of him, and yet he was like him, pinned to this ugly background, walled in, suffocating. "Did you ever think about therapy after it . . . you know . . ."

"Thought about a lot of things. Thought about telling someone, the police, a friend, but I had nothing to tell anyone, and I had no friends. It was just a lot of things in my head, nothing coherent."

"What do you really remember, Bruce?" He looked him in the eye.

Bruce took a breath.

"Take your time." August knew even talking about it distressed him, but he figured he wanted to do it now, maybe even needed to do it. He wouldn't have come otherwise.

Bruce met his gaze. "I remember the night he took us there to that place. It was really humid that night, hard to breathe. Tommy and I went for a swim and—"

August waited.

"When I came out of the water, I didn't see Tommy anymore. He was just . . . just gone."

"What did you do?"

"I dried off, and I went looking for him. I thought he was fooling around, playing a trick. He liked to do that stuff. I called his name, told him to smarten up. I walked away down the road, but I felt weird, spooked. Something wasn't quite right. I knew it. You ever get that feeling when you know something is wrong?"

"Yes. Sometimes."

"Then, suddenly, someone hit me on the head, hard. I went down on my knees, and the last thing I saw was the night sky fading to black."

August gripped the railing, his knuckles straining white. "This is as hard for me as it is for you somehow."

A hand covered his, caressed his knuckles. "I believe you," Bruce said softly.

August looked up, his eyes stinging with unshed tears.

Bruce brought his hand up around August's neck and squeezed. He moved closer. Bruce's hand felt good there, strong, supportive. He caressed August's hair with his fingers, their breaths mingling.

Bending his head, August pressed his forehead against Bruce's for a minute. "You're not alone anymore," he whispered.

Bruce nodded as August moved his mouth over his. With lips lightly caressing his, August mouthed, "It's okay, it's okay."

When August gasped and closed the gap between their mouths, Bruce clung to him for a moment, his mouth opening slightly, lips gently, tenderly tasting August as the kiss deepened.

The kiss went on for no more than thirty seconds before Bruce took a step back, putting some distance between them. August looked kind of stunned. Bruce reached out and touched his cheek. "I've probably wanted to do that since I first saw that picture of you," he smiled, "the one in your police uniform. I'm sorry if I crossed the line."

August shook his head. He smiled uneasily. "It's okay. I didn't put up much of a fight, did I?"

Bruce finally took care of the embarrassment by cracking a joke. "You're not telling me you're easy now, are you, August?"

"You got me," August put up his hands with a smirk, "I'm a real slut."

They both laughed and took the opportunity to create an even greater distance between them. August looked out at the trees and the mountains and knew that even if they laughed it off, they couldn't just erase what had happened.

He looked up in surprise when Bruce took up where he'd left off in his recounting of that fateful night. "When I opened my eyes again, my head was bleeding, but not too badly. It hurt like hell though, and I couldn't see much. It was dark, and it smelled bad in there, damp, musty. I could hear someone moaning not too far away. He was trying to cry out, but it sounded muffled like he had a gag in his mouth."

"But not in yours?"

"No. He had plans for me." Bruce clutched his coffee cup. He breathed in the air. "It's going to snow soon."

"Yes. I feel it. This is the last reprieve before the winter, the last taste of the sun."

"I want to go with you to town, visit these people who ran the campgrounds, okay?"

"Sure." He guessed that was as far as Bruce could go today, but that was all right. He knew that he'd tell him more when he was ready. It was enough for both. "Let's have some breakfast and then we'll go."

"You cooking?"

"Are you afraid?"

Bruce followed him inside. "Not with you."

August turned to look at him now. He knew Bruce wasn't talking about his cooking.

As they drove, Bruce scanned the surroundings. "There's the house we rented over there across the lake." He pointed into the distance as the car whizzed by.

"It's no longer a rental. The owners decided to live in it permanently now. They've retired there."

"They worked for the airline, right?"

"Yes, Mr. Jackson was a commercial pilot. His wife used to travel everywhere with him. They've been all over the world."

"Wow. Would you like that, to travel all the time?"

"No," August said. "I'd hate it. I just want to live in one place, go to work, come home, and see the same face sitting across from me at night . . . hold the same person in my arms each night when I go to bed. "

Bruce swallowed. He turned his gaze to him. Oh God, that's all he wanted, too, the simple life, great sex, maybe even a little crazy sex with someone who knew what to hell they were doing in bed, with someone who really cared about him. To laugh, share a glass of wine, watch a good movie curled up in each other's arms, and no more fucking nightmares.

Stop it, Bruce, it's never going to happen. I won't let it happen.

When August looked at him, Bruce looked away. He didn't want him to see what was in his eyes. He was almost afraid that August could read his thoughts.

Don't do this. Don't talk to me.

They drove in silence along the lake and into the town. The video store was still there on the corner where he and Tommy used to come on their bicycles, and Tommy used to rent all those bloody cop movies. A few doors down was the hamburger stand. It was closed for the season. As they drove on, Bruce spotted the bandstand which was a historical landmark built on the common, and several Victorian-style inns and hotels, including the Mountain View House which stood on the hilltop. "Did you know that the Mountain View House is said to be the most luxurious hotel in New Hampshire?" Bruce said.

"Apparently," August said, turning down a side street toward the lake.

"Ever stay there?"

"No. You?"

"No, but I always wanted to. My mother said it was too expensive."

"This is where they live," August announced as he pulled up to the curb in front of a cute little brick bungalow perched on the edge of the shore. He turned off the engine and got out of the car.

Bruce joined him, looking around cautiously. "I'll let you do the talking. I'm sure they don't remember me. We only rented that cottage for a few months before . . . well . . ."

August nodded. "Don't worry."

The man who opened the door was stooped some. He had snow-white hair, and when August told him his name, he had to repeat it twice. His wife was very sharp and came forward immediately. She remembered August and his mother. "I was very sad when your mother passed away, August," she said as they sat on the sofa in the modestly decorated living room. "She was far too young to die." She served them tea and little shortbread biscuits.

The old man sat in a chair nearby, but he really couldn't hear what they said. He nodded and smiled, sometimes answering a question that was never asked.

August had introduced Bruce as his friend, but he didn't go into more detail than that. He wondered if that was really what they were, friends . . . Or were they just tragically connected? Or, could it be something more than that? He couldn't help but remember what August's mouth had felt like on his. He could still taste the sweetness. He told himself to forget it, to concentrate on what Mrs. Curby was saying.

"I appreciated the flowers you sent," August said graciously. "Mother loved gladiolas."

"Took them from the garden." She nodded. "She always came by to admire the flowers. It's nice of you to come to visit, dear. Are you staying up at the lake?"

"For a little while." August put down his cup. "Mrs. Curby, there is another reason I stopped by. I was wondering if you kept records of those campers who rented space in the campgrounds when you were running it."

"Yes," she said. "We always made them sign the register."

"Do you still have those books?"

"Oh my." She placed a hand to her breast. "We packed all that stuff away, dear. How far back are you talking?"

"Ten years, or more."

"Ten years. I couldn't tell you where you would find those ones," she laughed a little, "but you young fellows are welcome to go up into the attic and go through the stuff we packed. Take what you want."

August looked at Bruce, and Bruce nodded. "Let's do it," he said.

A half hour later, they were tearing into boxes in the dusty attic, the only light coming from the dirt-encrusted window. "What are we looking for again?" Bruce asked.

August sat on the floor, checking each register. "May, June and July two-thousand and nine especially, but anything in that year is good. Find all the registers in that year and put them in that pile there. We'll take them back to the house and go through them. The dust up here is getting to me now."

For the next three hours, they worked side by side, sorting the registers the Curby's had kept for over thirty-two years. Finally, they repacked everything in the boxes, except the registers they'd put aside.

Mrs. Curby had prepared supper, and she insisted they stay. They ate delicious home-made clam chowder and thick water bread, followed by chocolate pudding with whipped cream. Mr. Curby went on about the low-class campers who now frequented Roger's Campground in a too-loud voice, while Mrs. Curby smiled indulgently at him.

Both men thanked the Curby's for their hospitality an hour or so later and said their goodbyes. Bruce knew that August was anxious to go through those books. He took the registries and dumped them into the trunk of the car. It was dark outside now, and August stood looking at the night sky a few seconds. He commented that it was snowing, and then climbed into the driver's seat. Starting the motor, he let it warm up a bit, and turned on the wipers. Bruce looked at the snowflakes settling in August's thick black hair. They looked like crystals.

"It's pretty," Bruce said. He had an urge to touch August's hair and brush away the snow.

"Pretty?" August snorted. "It's freezing."

Bruce smiled. "I like it." There was something comforting about the snow. He always felt safer in the winter; as if no one could ever hurt him unless the sun was heating up the water.

"You don't even have a decent winter coat," August muttered as he brought his foot down on the gas and they started on their way back.

Bruce shrugged. He didn't feel the cold. It was nice and warm in the car. "Do you think we'll find anything useful in those books?" Bruce asked as August rolled through main street.

"Do you want to?"

"What does that mean?"

"I don't know. Maybe it's better if we don't."

"If you thought that, you would have left me in Montreal."

August didn't answer.

"But you think we will find something because of me?"

"Yes."

The snow had melted on August's hair. It was damp in some places; a piece of it fell over his forehead. "I hope I don't disappoint you."

"You won't."

"Why do you think the police closed the case? They must have reopened it now because of that kid."

"I don't know if they've reopened Tommy's murder investigation."

"Have you spoken to the police since then?"

"On several occasions, but without getting much information. They speculated that it's a copycat crime." Bruce fell silent.

"If we can gather any evidence that can tie Tommy's murder to the present crime, maybe they'll reopen that case."

"Do you think it's the . . ." He paused, then forged on.

"Do you think it's *him*?"

August pulled up into the driveway in front of the house. "Yes, I do." The wind had really kicked up. August turned off the motor, grabbed the piles of books in the trunk and ran up to the door, struggling to get his key in the lock.

Bruce chuckled as they walked inside. "You really don't like the cold."

"Look at you. At least I have a leather coat. I'd be freezing my butt off."

Bruce nodded. "Okay. I need a job so that I can get a coat. Think I can get one?"

"Maybe. You plan on sticking around?" August eyed him.

Bruce shrugged. "For now. You need me, don't you?"

"Yeah, I need you."

"Okay. Well, I've got to earn some cash."

"What about your mother?" August asked as he locked up the front door and went into the living room. He dropped the books on the coffee table and went into the kitchen. "Don't you think you should call her, let her know you're here?"

"It's just that . . ."

"It's just that what?" August shrugged off his coat as he came back into view. "She's going to find out you're here sooner or later."

"I know. It's just that she'll ask a lot of questions."

"Maybe it's time you answered them."

"Not just yet, okay. Soon." He sat down on the sofa and picked up the first book. "Let's get started, shall we?"

"Okay, I've put on some coffee."

"We're going to need it."

"They're all in order," August told him, sitting down beside him on the sofa. "Try to keep them that way, okay?"

"Sure."

"Here's some paper and a pen. Mark down every time you see a name more than once, with the date."

Bruce took the paper and went to work. They drank up almost the full twelve cups of coffee that was in the carafe and then realized that it was after two in the morning. "Find anything?" August asked.

"There are over one hundred spaces for trailers. That's not even counting tents. There are some people who come every weekend, others who spend the entire summer.

It's complicated."

"I didn't find the book for July of that year in this stack. Did you?"

"No. I didn't," Bruce replied. "Maybe the police confiscated it for evidence."

"No, they gave everything back,' August told him.

"Think we just didn't see it back at the house?"

"No, I had it earlier."

"Then it's missing?" Bruce looked stunned.

"Looks like it. Shit, I know I put it in the pile. Maybe I dropped it somewhere."

"We've done this all for nothing then."

"No, I know I had it. I'll have to look for it tomorrow," August groaned, sitting back on the sofa and rubbing his eyes. "I'm just too tired. Let's leave it for tonight, and go to bed, okay?"

"Sounds like a plan." Bruce stood. "See you in the morning."

August nodded. "Night."

August bolted upright in bed. The sounds wafting down the corridor and into his room sounded like a wounded animal. He shook the sleep from his eyes and got out of bed. The noise was coming from Bruce's room. "Jesus." He hurried down the darkened hallway and opened the door, moving quickly over to the bed where Bruce lay thrashing, the blankets huddled at the bottom of the bed. The window was wide open, the cold air pouring in and making the room feel like a deep freeze. August quickly went to close it, then came back to the bed.

"Bruce," he said gently, then a little louder as he placed his hands on his shoulders to quiet him. "Stop it, wake up. You're okay. You're safe."

Bruce sat up and went right into his arms. He was shaking like a leaf as he clutched onto him, his body wet with sweat despite the freezing room. He hugged him so tightly, August could hardly breathe. He had to wrestle a bit with his arms, causing Bruce to relax his hold. "It's all right. It's okay."

Bruce sobbed on his shoulder, and August stroked his back, rocking him a little as one might a baby. Then he caressed his hair, and the baby-soft fineness of it felt like silk between his fingers.

"August, don't leave me," he moaned. "Please."

"Bruce, it's freezing in here. Why was the window open? Did you open it?"

"I don't know," he muttered. "I didn't open it. Don't leave me. Stay with me," he whispered as August felt his lips press against his shoulder. A hand moved down his back and over his lap.

August sucked in some breath as Bruce's hand moved over the hardness in his underwear. When had he gotten an erection? Maybe he'd woken up with it or maybe being here in this room, holding a near-naked Bruce in his arms in the middle of the night, had spurred it.

Bruce's fingers strayed over his cock, measuring its girth blindly through the material. "You're beautiful," he whispered. "Stay here," he moaned, moving his mouth up August's throat to his jaw, "stay here with me and fuck me."

Fingers curled around his shaft now, still cushioned by the material of his briefs. He suddenly longed for Bruce to touch the hot flesh underneath. He snaked his hand down to the waistband of his briefs as Bruce's tongue met his and lifted his sex out over the waistband.

Bruce sighed into his mouth, his fingers now truly fondling his cock. He grunted something and pushed August down on the bed. He leaned over, with August's feet still on the floor and ran his tongue up the length of August's shaft. August's fingers tightened on the sheets as Bruce grasped the base of August's cock in his fist and sucked the head into his mouth. August lifted his hips in invitation, and his hand came down again on that baby fine hair.

Bruce took him deeper into his mouth, and August pulled at his hair. *Jesus God . . . suck, suck. Yes. Um . . . yes . . .*

August moaned, and Bruce began to move his lips and his tongue, sucking and bobbing in earnest as August's entire body trembled on the brink of orgasm. "Oh fuck!" he cried out. His entire body went into spasm as Bruce reared back, and he blew a stream of cum up over his belly and onto Bruce's chest.

Bruce went down into his arms, kissing his mouth again hotly, rubbing his hands over August's chest and arms. August rolled onto the bed with him. His mind had shut down, his body was on automatic. There was only this moment, only the sounds of pleasure and urgency as August pressed Bruce to the mattress and began to lick each nipple, his hand sliding down his stomach to his thigh and in between his legs.

August bit and suckled his nipples while Bruce bucked his hips and sliced his hand through August's hair. August's mouth moved down Bruce's belly to his cock, which was hard and impatiently in need of attention. He licked the head, and Bruce cried out. He took it into his mouth, fondling Bruce's balls and then teasing his finger along the sensitive rosebud deep within the cheeks of his ass.

"Oh God, August," he whimpered. "Fuck!"

August released his cock and then flipped him over. He tongued his hole, holding his ass cheeks open, and then inserted the tip of his finger.

Bruce slammed his fist on the mattress.

"You like that?" August asked.

"Um, yeah . . . deeper, come on."

August slowly inserted his finger to the knuckle then pushed harder. He reached under and played with Bruce's cock a little, licked his balls and then pushed two fingers up inside of him. One hook and he found what he wanted. Bruce moaned deeply, and he kept moaning as August fucked him with his fingers.

"Your cock," Bruce gasped. "Fuck me with that cock of yours. God, I dreamt about it tonight. Come on, come on, baby."

"Condoms? I don't think . . ."

"In my bag," he grunted. "On the floor. I have some and lube. Under the bed."

August pulled out his fingers. He hung over the bed and reached for the bag. He felt Bruce's hands run over his ass as he did. He brought up the bag and searched around blindly in the dark. He found the lube, and Bruce took it from him. "Put the rubber on," he breathed.

August ripped open the package while Bruce got up on all fours and spread lube on his hands.

"That's my job," August said softly after he'd put on the condom. He rubbed his hands over Bruce's and then pushed him back into position. "You want to be fucked like that?"

"Yeah," he breathed. "Yeah, just like that, deep and hard. Do it, do it, August. Fuck me. "

August inserted his slippery fingers up inside his hole, lubricating it well. Bruce squirmed and groaned a little, pressing his hand to his ass once when August was going to remove it. "Wait," he sighed. "Wait. God, that feels so good. You have the touch. Um, yeah . . . that hook, you know the spot . . . . Oh, shit I'm going to come. Come on, take me. I'm yours, August. Take me."

August gripped his hips and pressed the head of his cock up inside of his ass. He closed his eyes as he felt his shaft sink deeper in his tight, hot tunnel. He let his head go back and pumped into Bruce, lifting one of his legs and fucking him on an angle at one point in order to get even deeper.

He lost himself, bucking harder and faster, grabbing a fistful of Bruce's hair at one point and yanking his head around for a deep, all-encompassing kiss. He was gone. He'd never felt so ferocious, so feral. Something in Bruce brought it out in him. Passion released, and it felt as if he could fuck Bruce's ass all night long.

When he finally came, he thought his heart would break out of his chest. It was beating so loudly, and so hard he was sure he was having a heart attack. He came with a shout, Bruce's leaking, dwindling cock shooting in between his fingers.

He pulled out of the man and lay on his back, trying to catch his breath. His body was slick with sweat, and he was still trying to recover as Bruce moved closer to him and laid his head on his shoulder.

They didn't speak. Neither of them had the energy really. And maybe it was better if they didn't.

A few minutes later, Bruce moved his hand over August's chest and brushed his cock a few times. "You're hard again." This man was a marvel.

You want him again, don't you? You want his cock inside of you.

August lifted his head and glanced at his cock. "I see that."

"Can I suck it?" He so wanted to. He hadn't had enough yet.

You slut! You're a real whore but then with a man like that . . .

August laughed and turned his head to look at him.

"If you have the energy."

"God damn it, August, you're so hot. Don't you know that? I don't know how any guy you're fucking could ever get any sleep."

August smiled.

"Who was the last one?" Bruce asked, his fingers now handling his balls. Suddenly, he wanted to know.

He's had many. He won't even remember your little ass when he's through.

August closed his eyes. "Keep that up. That feels . . . um . . . yeah . . ."

"Shut up," Bruce muttered as he kissed his shoulder.

"Was he hot?" He massaged his balls in his hand, pushing them together and then apart. He wanted to swallow him whole.

"Yeah. He was hot. Why did you tell me to shut up?"

"I didn't forget it." *God, did I say that aloud?* "Did you fuck him the way you did me just now?"

"Not exactly."

Bruce turned his face to his. "Was it good tonight?"

"Oh yeah," he moaned. "It was good." He turned to him and pulled him closer, kissing his mouth hotly.

He's just saying that. He wants to get laid.

Bruce ran his hand over August's hair. His other hand worked the man's cock, which was halfway to right where he wanted it. He blocked out the voice. His vision was filled with August. "Will you fuck me again?" Bruce grunted as they rolled together on the bed.

August looked down into his eyes, one leg over his. Bruce could feel his hardness, his need. Bruce licked his lips. *He wants me.* "Fuck me again."

"God damn it," August swore. He lifted Bruce's legs up over his shoulders and yanked his hips up off the bed.

"Look at me. Look at me, baby, look into my eyes."

"I'm looking." *I really think I love him.*

August struggled with a fresh rubber. Bruce took it from him and rolled it onto August's cock. He was a big guy, broad shoulders, all muscle, and that cock, standing straight out right now was the most beautiful he'd ever seen. "I want to ride that cock. Come on, baby," he urged. "Make me feel it. Make me feel alive."

August slapped his ass with both hands once and then seized his hips. He wiggled into just the right spot and then took him, possessed him with his cock in a way Bruce had never been possessed before. He wanted to stay there with August's big, thick cock inside his ass, spreading him wide, stretching him to the limit, and then bringing him home like none other. He reached up and gripped the headboard. He watched August's face contort, and the muscles in his body strain as he worked his hips back and forth, driving that cock home.

Bruce worked with him, moving his body in such a way as to take him even deeper. His eyes closed as the earth around him shattered. He cried out as his cock released his load, spraying August's chest and his face. August came himself, slamming the last few thrusts of passion into Bruce.

He didn't separate from him, however. Instead, he lowered Bruce's legs around his slim hips and pulled him up onto his lap. Bruce's arms went around August's neck, and they kissed, slowly, sensuously, touching each other without urgency.

August's softened cock was still inside of him. It felt good there. He didn't want to disconnect. He looked into those eyes and saw something he didn't think he'd ever see. He hugged him close while August's arms closed around him, holding him tight. They stayed like that for a while and then August let him down, making that disconnection.

Bruce watched him.

I see you, Bruce. You see how easily he can leave you. Ask him. You want to.

"Did you fuck him in Montreal?"

August turned to look at him. "What?"

"The last one? Did you fuck him in Montreal?"

He doesn't care about you really. But we'll always be together.

"Forget about that, okay?" he said. "Who opened the window?"

"I don't know. I thought you did, and you forgot to close it."

"No," August said, examining the window. "No one has tampered with it. Strange. I would have never opened it this time of the year. I didn't even come in here."

"Yeah, forget it." He turned over in bed. "I'm going to get some sleep. Are you going to sleep here?" He waited for an answer.

"No," August said and left the room.

You see, Bruce. What did I tell you? He's had you, and he's tired of you already.

Chapter Six

A ugust tried to sleep but couldn't. He was going to have to do something about this insomnia. He went back to the books that the Curbys' had diligently kept and wondered where in the hell the one for July had disappeared to. He was sure he'd seen it in the attic, put it in the pile with the others. It was like, nowhere.

At the time of Tommy's murder, the people in Whitefield and Lancaster had a tough time telling police if they'd noticed any strange, suspicious people around. It was, after all, tourist session, and the town was filled with strangers at that time.

August wanted to go to talk to the family whose son had just been murdered. Maybe they knew something that could be tied in to Tommy's murder. But he felt it was too soon for that. They needed time to grieve.

He sat on the sofa and pulled a scrapbook out from under the coffee table. He set it on his lap and opened it. He looked at the newspaper clippings about his brother's murder and saw his brother's faded photograph staring back at him. Maybe it had been a local, someone here right in town. Shit. Surely Bruce could remember more than what he'd told him about that man who had handed Tommy the photograph from the bushes that day.

Bruce. Had he made a mistake fucking him like that? It would change everything, but then again, they both needed something. What was the harm? Except that it was more than just a fuck. He knew it, and he suspected that Bruce knew it too. It was intense, almost surreal. There was a connection like he'd never known before and that made him very uncomfortable.

He yawned, curled up on the sofa, and closed the scrapbook. He shut his eyes and fell asleep.

Bruce glanced in the mirror after he washed his face.

You have a face, Bruce. But I have no face. I've never had a face.

Bruce dropped the towel in the sink. He swallowed, left the bathroom and walked into the kitchen. "August?" No answer.

Panic ran through him. "August?" He walked into the living room. "Where are you?"

"Here," a voice replied.

Bruce sighed in relief as he saw him walk through the door. He ran over and hugged him tight, kissing his cheek. He was cold. "Where were you? I was worried."

"Worried about what?" August laughed, taking off his coat.

"Where did you go?"

"Just to check out a few things. I spoke with Desmond at the police station."

"Desmond?"

"Yeah, we went to school together. He's a friend, a cop. I told him that—"

"You didn't tell him about me, did you? About me being back here?"

"No, but, Bruce, people are going to know eventually."

"People don't know I was with Tommy that night."

"Yeah, and we need to talk about that."

"I'm not ready to go to the police."

"It's been ten years."

"I . . . I need to get things straight in my mind; that's all."

"You should go and see your mother." August sat down on the sofa.

"Will you get over me going to see my mother?" He heard the anger in his voice. He felt a flash of regret when he saw August's surprise. "I'm sorry, I'm sorry, baby," he said softly. He came over and sat beside him. "This is a lot for me right now. I'd rather tell you first, and then we can see the police and my mother."

"Okay," August said, but he still looked perplexed.

"Don't you miss your mother a little?"

He shrugged. "I was never close to her. I guess that's why I spent so much time with Tommy that summer, and practically lived here." He smiled. "My mother is an academic, was never warm and nurturing like yours, you know? There was a lot of fighting and conflict in the house."

"I understand. And you never mentioned your dad. What happened to him?"

"I don't know." He shook his head. "My mother never talked about him much. Either he died, or he just cut out. I've heard both versions. You think my mother is still here in town?"

August narrowed his eyes. "You mean you don't know?"

"We were always moving around when I was younger. I really doubt she's still in Whitefield. She doesn't like to stay in one place."

"Bruce, why didn't your mother ever report you missing? I find that weird. I mean you were still underage. She never reported it to the police. Did you call her to say you were all right?"

"Yeah. I did. I kept telling her I was coming home. I said I needed space. I've always been independent. She knew I'd be okay." He stood up. "I'm starved, let's eat."

August made a late breakfast, and they ate side by side at the kitchen table, each with their own thoughts. He'd checked this morning, and Bruce's mother, Evelyn Monkton, was still in the phonebook, and she was listed as the principle of Whitefield Elementary on the school website. He was going to go back to see the Curbys today and see if he'd perhaps dropped that missing book somewhere. Maybe he could dig up some more information about the last murder. He and Desmond were supposed to have lunch today.

He told Bruce he had some things to do and left the house. He really didn't want to go into detail. He met Desmond at the diner, and they ordered the special, a club sandwich on brown bread with fries and gravy. Not the healthiest thing, but he was hungry.

Desmond still looked at him the way he'd done when they were an item. It was unsettling. To August, it was eons ago and better left in the past. They'd gone to the academy together. Desmond was good-looking, and he knew it, although he wasn't much to write home about in bed that August remembered, rather, he was Mr. Lie-there-and-let-the other-guy-do-all-the-work. He was a hotshot and wanted to be a big city detective, but down deep, he wasn't a bad guy. Their affair had been secretive and short-lived. Desmond was destined to stay in the closet, and August was desperate to get out of one.

Miraculously, Desmond had ended up here in Whitefield. August had been as surprised as Desmond when they'd run into each other after August's mother had died. Although he hadn't been the investigator on the case when Tommy was murdered, the case being before his time, he'd been great ever since August had come to him after Washington was killed. He said he'd do what he could to reopen the investigation.

Desmond was a smart cop, even if he was a bit of macho man with a huge ego. He'd been good about sharing information with him about this case. "It was a trip, man," he said now, chewing on a fry as August sipped his coffee, "finding that head. I don't think I'll ever forget it."

That made August shiver. "Anything else since then?"

"Actually, yeah. There is something, although it's probably nothing. Apparently, right after the murder of Washington Jones, some insomniac with his dog said he saw a guy in a dark sweater and jeans walking along Main Street. He said he could swear he had some sort of an axe or something in his hand, but he couldn't be sure. He was holding it in front of him as he walked. He thought it odd though that this guy was on the street because it was like three in the morning, you know?"

"What did he look like? Was he close enough to ID him?"

"He said he was blond, in his twenties, about five eleven, thin."

"Had he ever seen him before?"

"No."

"Not much to go on." August shook his head. "Ten years, Des. Ten years, nothing. Then, boom, and it happens back here, in this place. The question is why."

"It's strange," he muttered and called to the waitress to bring more coffee. "Hell, if I knew why, I'd be done with all these homicides. They're all the same, so it's pretty obvious that they were committed by the same guy or a copycat killer, but yet, he covers his tracks. No one sees anything. He kills, and then just disappears into thin air, like some sort of a ghost."

"Hmm." August took a second cup of coffee as well.

"You look good," Desmond said suddenly.

"Thanks."

"You here for a while?"

"Yeah, maybe."

"You're not playing cop, are you?"

"I am a cop."

He laughed. "You were a cop."

"Technicality."

"I'm not immune to the irony that this Washington killing brought you home."

"Big words. You been studying the dictionary again?" August smirked.

"Very funny. Don't flirt with me, boy." He leaned forward and lowered his voice. "I've got more than one weapon in my pants."

August laughed out loud. "Be still my heart."

He grinned. "So, stop teasing me, and come home with me. I can take off a few hours, and we can get to know each other again."

"Some other time, okay?"

He sat back, drained his coffee. "If you're going to pump me for information, August, you better be prepared to pump me in other ways." He lifted his eyebrows and grinned.

"I'll get the check, how's that?" August asked, shaking his head.

"Torture," he mouthed.

They both laughed and broke apart outside the diner, going their separate ways. As August walked up the street, he spotted something out of the corner of his eye. He saw a flash of pale blond hair as a face looked out at him from across the street. *Bruce?* How did he get to town? August skipped across the street, dodging a few cars and called out to him. "Bruce?" He arrived breathless in the alley where he'd seen him, but he was like nowhere.

August looked around and shivered. Had he imagined it?

He continued up the street then stopped in front of the Washington house. There was a for sale sign on the front yard. He took a breath and walked up the path. He hesitated a moment and then rang the bell.

He's fucking that cop. If you think he'll be yours forever, think again. Nothing is forever, Bruce, you know that. Remember? If you forget, I'll take you down to Blood Pond and . . .

Bruce clutched the sideboard as he raised his eyes to the mirror.

You have a face. I have no face.

Stop it. Stop it. Just fucking stop it!

He whirled around, grabbed the lamp on the sideboard and threw it at the mirror. It shattered into several pieces. He picked up one of the shards and stared at it.

Do it. Do it.

He dropped it onto the carpet. He looked around the room. He needed a drink. Where in hell did August keep his liquor?

Martha Jones opened the door. She looked pale and haggard. A little girl, about seven years old with pigtails, rushed to the door as well. She clung to her mother and peered at August curiously. "Martha?" he said. "I guess you don't remember me but—"

"August? August Greystone. Of course. I remember you. How are you?"

"Fine. I was wondering if we might talk about Washington."

She hesitated and then nodded. "Ally, honey, run upstairs and play with your dolls, okay? Come in, August."

August walked into a house in disarray.

"Sorry, we're selling the house and . . ."

The little girl peeked at him from behind the rail and then disappeared upstairs. "It's okay," he said. "Where you going?"

"I'm moving back with my folks in Newport."

"Oh." He didn't want to pry. "I'm sorry."

She shrugged and cleared a chair for him to sit in the living room. There were boxes everywhere. "Can I get you a cola or something?"

"No. Thanks. Martha, what can you tell me about the night Washington was murdered?"

"He phoned about four in the afternoon. He was working at the campgrounds for the summer, cleaning up the grounds. He was really proud of that job." She swallowed.

August touched her hand.

"I feel like you understand." The tears ran silently down her face.

"I do."

"What did he say on the phone?"

"He said he wouldn't be home for supper. He met a friend, some friend he had at the campground, and they were going to —"

"Who was this friend? Did you ever meet him? Did he tell you his name?"

"I never saw this boy. He was camping, I guess, and they hit it off, used to swim together after work. Washington was always a shy kid. We were glad he had a friend."

"That night, the camp director said he saw Washington head off around four-thirty up the Turtle Brook Trail. He was alone when the director saw him. The director said he never saw him with anyone, that there was no boy at the campgrounds at that time who would have been around Washington's age."

"Could he have been making him up?" August asked.

"He wouldn't have lied about that. And one night I came downstairs and heard Washington talking to someone out back. There were two voices. When I called to him, he came inside. When I asked him who he was talking to, he said 'Bruce.'"

August's jaw dropped. "What?"

"He said he'd been talking to Bruce. That's all I know."

The strangest sensation crept over him. Of course, there were many Bruce's in the world. It couldn't have been Bruce Monkton.

"Are you all right, August?"

He stood. "Sure. And no one ever saw them together that you know of?"

She shook her head. "I know it sounds like he made this guy up, but he talked about him like he was real." She stood up, too.

He gave her a hug. "I'm sorry about Washington. If I find out anything to help the police, I'll let you know."

She hurried to the desk. "Here's my number in Newport." She scribbled it on a piece of paper. "Call me."

"I will."

August was still thinking about what Martha Jones had told him as he pulled up in front of the summer house. As soon as he got out, he knew something was wrong. The door was wide open for one thing. He walked in cautiously and looked around. When he entered the living room, he gasped. There was broken glass everywhere, and the living room furniture had been tipped over.

"Bruce?"

Nothing. He'd just begun to put the room back together when the phone rang.

He swore and went to pick it up. "Mr. Greystone," the voice said on the other end of the line, "it's Mrs. Monkton, Bruce's mother. I've been told you have my boy there."

"Bruce is here, yes."

"I want you to send him home."

"That's his decision, Mrs. Monkton. I've been trying to encourage him to—"

"Just get him home now!" The phone went dead.

"What the hell!" He heard a noise suddenly, and he turned around to see Bruce. It was all he could do just to stand up, and he held a half-empty bottle of something in his hand. He lifted it.

"Hey, beautiful," he slurred. "You want a drink?"

"Jesus Christ," August muttered, "you're absolutely toasted." He walked over and took the bottle out of Bruce's hand.

Bruce tried to throw his arms around him. "Want to fuck?"

"Yeah, right," August replied. "Come on, let's get you upstairs. What the hell is going on with you? Did you smash the mirror?"

"No, not me," he slurred as August pulled him down the hall toward the bedroom. "It wasn't me. I didn't listen this time. I didn't . . ."

"Okay, okay." August got him onto the bed. "Sleep it off."

"August." Bruce reached out to him.

August looked down at him. "What?"

"Be careful, okay? I couldn't . . . I couldn't bear it if something happened to you."

"Nothing is going to happen to me. Close your eyes."

"Stay with me. Don't leave me alone."

August lowered his head to Bruce's chest, concern furrowing his brow. "I won't, baby, I won't."

He waited until Bruce fell asleep and then he got up.

As Bruce slept, August paced. His mind raced with all the possibilities. Could Bruce have killed Washington? He was somewhere in New Hampshire at the time it happened. There was a period where August couldn't catch up to him. If he killed Washington, had he killed Tommy, too?

"God, God," he moaned, putting his face in his hands. He couldn't face that. Had he slept with his brother's killer?

He tried to sleep, but he just lay there for hours. Then he got up and walked back into Bruce's room. He quietly searched the drawers, under the bed, and then his bag. At the bottom of his knapsack, he drew out a small book. It was one of the registries from the campground, the one dated July 2009.

August closed his eyes. The panic was now setting in. How could he have been so stupid? He took the book and went to the living room. He sat down on the sofa and opened it. He ran his finger down the row of signatures, stopping suddenly when he saw the July second entry. *Clay Monkton*. His name appeared for the next two weeks, disappearing the night of Tommy's murder. The entry indicated that he'd rented a tent and pitched it in the most remote area of the wooded campgrounds. *Clay Monkton*. It was Bruce's middle name, and the name he used when he was running.

He dropped the book on the floor when a shadow fell across him. He looked up to find Bruce standing in front of him. "You're afraid of me, aren't you, August?"

"No," August replied. "I'm not afraid. Why did you hide the book?"

"Because I saw that name there. I didn't write that name, August. You got to believe me. Why in hell would I have stayed at the campgrounds when my mother had rented that house? It wouldn't have made sense."

"Then why were you using that name when I found you? Who are you trying to protect?"

"I'm not protecting anyone, and it's my middle name. It was normal that I'd use it if I was hiding from someone."

"Who are you hiding from? Me, a killer, yourself? Who, Bruce? If you don't tell me, I can't help you."

"Okay, so I should have told you that I hid the book, but I knew you'd think the worst when you saw it and—"

"Think the worst?" August stood now. "I come home to see you've wrecked the living room, broken a mirror, you've gotten drunk, and you've hidden the very thing you were supposed to help me look for! What in hell do you want me to think, Bruce?"

"I'll pay for the mirror and the—"

"Never mind that. Did you know Washington Jones?"

"The boy who was murdered? No. How could I have known him? Oh my God," he said, backing away. "You think I murdered him. You think I murdered Tommy, too!"

"I don't know what to think. I spoke to Martha Jones today. Washington went off to meet a friend the night he was killed, a friend that was supposed to be staying at the campgrounds, but no one ever saw them together. She said Washington called him Bruce."

"So, there are other guys called Bruce. Why not Clay, since that's the name I supposedly use to murder people?"

"Listen to me." August went over and took him by the shoulders. "I don't know what's going on." He tried to calm his voice. "Your mother called. She said she—"

"My mother?" He jerked away from him again. A look of real fear fell across his face. "What did she say? Does she know I'm here?"

"Yes. She knows. She wants you home. I—"

"Please, don't make me go there." He backed up against the wall. "If you make me go there, August, I'll ... run. You'll never see me again. I promise."

"No one is making you do anything." August put up his hands. "Calm down. You're a grown man. You don't have to go home. But if you want my help, you better start telling me the truth."

"You got to believe me, August," he said, "I didn't kill anyone. I swear on the night we spent together. Don't leave me."

August opened his arms, and Bruce went into them. He held him tight, not sure what in hell he was doing anymore. "I'm not going anywhere."

"Tell me you believe I didn't kill Tommy or Washington. Say it, August. Say it."

August looked down into his eyes. "I believe you," he said hesitantly, but down deep, he wasn't sure if that was true.

That night when August went to bed, Bruce followed him. He took off his clothes and crawled into bed beside him. "Please, baby, let me stay." August's body felt so warm and safe, and Bruce's desire for him was driving him half mad. When August started to respond to his touch, he blocked out everything in his mind, including the voice that told him August had been with the cop today.

Desmond wants him, and now he thinks you're a killer. There will always be that doubt in his mind.

You killed Tommy.

Bruce pushed August down on his back and pinned his arms above him. "Do you mind?" Bruce asked him. "Just a little play." He'd pulled the sash from August's housecoat, wrapped it around both his wrists and tied it to the rung in the headboard. "You won't get away now," he teased, on his knees between August's spread thighs.

"I wasn't going anyway," August replied, pulling at the constraints.

"That's sexy when you do that. Hmm." Bruce moved his hands down August's taut chest, tweaking each nipple, leaning down and nibbling one then the other. "You like that?"

"My cock likes that," August replied, meeting his eyes.

"You realize that you're my prisoner, my slave. I can do anything I want to you now." He pinched and pulled his nipples again, a little aggressively. August winced, but his cock rejoiced. Bruce kissed his belly and then licked the underside of August's erection. "I love your cock. It's so big and thick. Do you know what it feels like inside me?"

"No," he moaned, as Bruce began to lick and nibble at the shaft. "What does it feel like?"

"It fills my ass like a glove hugging a hand on a cold day. You're beautiful, August. Sometimes I look at you, and I see Tommy."

He took his cock into his mouth, sucking it hard and fast and then backed off, leaving August panting and breathless. He pushed August's thighs farther apart and lowered his head between his legs again. He licked his balls, tasted and teased them and then grabbed the lube. For a few minutes, he put on a show in front of him, greasing his own cock and then his nipples, making them hard. Then he reached under and inserted an oily finger up inside of August. His finger fucked him for a few minutes while August's head pressed back into the pillow and the chords stood out on his neck.

"Can I fuck you?" he pleaded, lowering his lips to August's left nipple. "I want to fuck you." He handled his cock again, and August grunted his agreement.

Bruce slipped on a condom.

Desmond fucked him today. They didn't eat at all.

They went to his apartment and played cops and robbers.

He put August down on all fours and fucked his ass well. He's not yours. There's only one way to make him yours completely.

Bruce went into him hard and fast.

August cried out as Bruce pumped. "Ah yes . . . yesssss . . . fucking . . . yeah!"

Bruce slowed his pace. Being inside him was heaven.

I've always wanted you, baby. Always. I never dreamed I'd be fucking you like this.

"August, baby, I'm coming, I'm coming." At the same time, he jerked August's beautiful big cock, and they came together, their bodies tingling with pleasure.

"Bruce," August said, "Untie me."

"Not yet."

"Do it, untie me," August insisted.

Bruce reached up and released the ties. "You're afraid of me, aren't you? Hold me," he whispered. He wanted to tell him that he thought he was in love, but he couldn't. It would probably freak August out, and Bruce knew that soon he'd have to leave here. It had been a mistake coming back, but he knew why he had come now. He'd come back for him, for August, for this moment of being in his big strong arms, where nothing could ever hurt him.

I want him.

Suddenly, Bruce jerked out of August's arms. He sprang up in the bed and screamed at the ceiling. "No! No! You can't have him. I'll never let you. I'll kill you first."

"Bruce! Bruce! Jesus Christ, who are you yelling at? There's no one here."

"He won't have you." Bruce turned and looked at him. He grabbed him and pulled him close. "I won't let him."

"Bruce." August struggled away from him. "What in hell are you talking about?"

"Did you fuck Desmond today?"

"Oh my God," he said, his face angry. "It was you. I swore I saw you in town today spying on me. How can you ask me that? Do you think I'd fuck Desmond after fucking you? And how do you know about him? You've been following me around? Jesus Christ, Bruce."

"It wasn't me." He shook his head.

"I saw you!" August yelled.

"I told you, it wasn't me." He got out of bed. "If you say you're not fucking Desmond, I believe you."

August didn't say anything. He just stared at him.

"I need something to drink. I'll be back."

August lay back down in the bed, stunned by Bruce's confession. Was he sick? Did he have multiple personalities? Something wasn't making sense. Tomorrow, he was going to go and see Bruce's mother. Maybe she could tell him what was happening. Bruce certainly wasn't telling him everything. He was having a hard time believing that Bruce could kill anyone, but maybe it was because he didn't want to believe it. He looked at him and thought, no, impossible, but after all that had happened, there was still this doubt that lurked deep inside of him.

Some people would say he'd been crazy tonight, letting Bruce tie him up like that. Truth was he still trusted him. But what if he really was a killer? *Damn it, August. Where was your head?* He knew damn well where it was. It was between his legs.

Bruce came back with ice cream and two spoons. He was all smiles. They ate the ice cream, and Bruce moved in between August's thighs and lay back on his chest. August stroked his hair. Maybe if he tried talking to him again, when he was relaxed . . .

"Are you ever going to tell me the rest of what happened the night you were taken?"

Bruce glanced back at him. "Yes. I will. But first," he took the ice cream container and put it on the floor, "kiss me. Make love to me again. God, I ache for you. I love fucking you, but when you fuck me, you take me somewhere beautiful and unforgettable. Fuck me, baby, fuck me." Bruce crawled on top of him before he could articulate any kind of objection. He was already hard as Bruce touched him, kissed him everywhere.

It didn't take long for Bruce to make him stop thinking altogether. While August rolled on the condom, Bruce jumped off the bed. "In the shower," he urged. "Fuck me there."

August followed him like a drunken man to the bottle. In the bathroom, Bruce turned on the shower and pulled August into the spray, touching him everywhere. August pushed him against the tile, face first and yanked his hips out at an angle. He spent some time playing in his ass with the lube while Bruce moved his hips seductively, moaning and pumping, and then August took him, impaling his ass with his cock, his lips coming down on his neck. Bruce was so fucking hot, and August was horny. "Mmm, my gorgeous little slut," he muttered, "with your hot ass."

Bruce seemed to like that. He responded by pinching his own nipples and letting his head fall back against August's shoulder, his cock jutting out against the tile. August fondled it roughly, slowing down his pace a little and jutting in from the left and the right. Bruce cried out. "Oh God, that feels good. Jesus, August, you're such a good fuck," he groaned. "Come, come for me, baby. Come in my ass."

August shot inside of him. His cock pulsed, causing his eyes to close then he pulled out. His body fell back against the tile. Bruce turned around in his arms and clung to him, pressing his softened cock against August's thigh. He clung to him until August suggested that they get out of the shower.

Wrapped in towels, they huddled together on the sofa. Bruce got up and fetched a blanket, and they put some old movie on the television. Bruce fell asleep twenty minutes into it, cuddled up to August's chest.

August glanced down at his sweet face and pushed back his damp hair from his forehead. He felt so protective of him, but he wished that he knew what he was supposed to be protecting him from. Maybe Bruce was a demon with the face of an angel. He pulled him closer, holding him tight. "God help me," he whispered. "Don't let me be in love."

CHAPTER SEVEN

August rose early the following morning and drove to town. He double-checked the address then pulled to a stop in front of the house. It was an old sprawling house at the very end of a dead-end street. There was a lot of land, and the neighbors were not too close. It was a Saturday so he knew Evelyn Monkton wouldn't be working. There was no car out front, but that didn't mean anything. Maybe she didn't have a car, or she'd parked it in the garage at the side of the house.

When he walked up onto the porch, he almost went through it. The porch was in bad need of repair, and several boards had almost rotted through. He felt guilty, like he was being disloyal to Bruce. He rang the bell and waited. When no one answered, he almost turned around and left, deciding that this was probably a bad idea. He waited a few more minutes then turned to go. Perhaps it was too early in the day, or it was the wrong house.

When the door opened, it opened no more than a crack, and the woman who opened it didn't look especially happy to see him. She was in her housecoat, her hair in disarray. She looked as if she'd been sleeping. Maybe he'd woken her. "Mrs. Monkton?"

"Yes?" She didn't open the storm door.

"I'm August Greystone. We spoke on the phone."

"I know who you are."

"I'm sorry. Maybe this is a bad time. I'd like to talk to you about Bruce."

She didn't say anything.

"Is this a good time or . . ." He trailed off, feeling unsure.

She disappeared for a moment, closing the door again. Then suddenly, it opened again, and she peered at him.

"Don't come here anymore. I'll call you." The door closed again.

He stood there, stunned. There was rudeness, and then there was rudeness. He started down the front steps again, avoiding the rotten boards. He was surprised when the door opened again. "August?"

He turned and waited. He had no idea they were on a first name basis.

She came outside onto the porch, quietly closing the door behind her. It was cold out, and she wrapped the fuzzy pink housecoat around her tightly. When she spoke, she bent at her waist so that her voice would carry directly to his ear. "Bruce needs to come home. Send him home, August, if only for your own security."

"My security?"

"I'm sorry to have to tell you this because I suppose you've grown rather fond of him. He can be very endearing, but my son is a very sick young man. He has been under psychiatric care in the past. He doesn't take his medication, and he should be institutionalized. You shouldn't listen to him when he rambles. He can say some bizarre things. If you care about him, help me to get him the care he needs. Send him home."

"Mrs. Monkton, frankly I'm surprised at your sudden interest and concern for Bruce. When he ran away from home after my brother's death, you didn't even report him missing or try to find out why he ran."

"Bruce and I were constantly in touch."

"He told me that, but still, he was a little young to be on his own."

"We take care of our family our own way, Mr. Greystone." It was back to that.

"Anyway, at that time, it was good that he was away. Now he needs to come home."

"He needs to talk to the police and tell them what happened that night."

"There's no need to involve the police. He doesn't know anything that can help you. I'm sorry about your brother but . . . Look, August, Bruce won't come home willingly, so you tell me when and where, and I'll make sure he's taken care of by the right people."

August narrowed his brows. *The right people?*

She turned, went back inside the house, and closed the door again.

August walked back to his car. Psychiatric care?

Was she trying to cover up the murders he'd committed?

Did she know?

August went back to see Mrs. Curby again. He had the book from July 2009, and he asked her about the entries. "Do you remember a Clay Monkton?"

She pursed her lips, looking at the scribbles on the pages. "Camped way out in the woods," she mused. "Wait a minute. I'll ask Jacob. Even though his short-term memory is going, he can remember things way back." She went into the other room to speak to her husband. August could hear her talking loudly. "Do you remember? His name was Clay . . . Clay Monkton . . . camped way out in the woods. Didn't you remark about that to me at the time?"

The old man was saying something, and Mrs. Curby came back out into the hallway. "Jesse said the man wasn't too talkative. A middle-aged man . . . paid in all dollar bills."

"Middle-aged? Is he sure?"

"That's what he said, and something about having a dragon tattoo on his arm."

"Thanks, Mrs. Curby," August replied.

On the way back to the summer house, he thought about what Mr. Curby had said. *He was a middle-aged man with a dragon tattoo on his arm.* He could have been in the army or in some sort of biker gang. But why would he have signed his name Clay Monkton? That part he still didn't get. It was beginning to resemble some sort of a sick joke?

Bruce was sitting on the sofa, staring at a blank television set when August finally walked into the house. He watched silently as August took off his coat and hung it up. It wouldn't be long now, and he'd have to leave him. He didn't want to this time. The thought of it caused him more grief than he really knew what to do with. He was already deeply in love with August, although right now, he was hurt and angry that August had seen his mother behind his back.

"Why did you go to my mother's?" he asked the moment August stepped into the living room. "You promised you wouldn't make me go home. You accuse me of lying, but then you do the same thing."

"Your mother says you're sick. She says you need some help and—"

"She's lying. August. I thought you would trust me. I thought that you'd believe me."

"I only want what's best for you, and you won't talk to me. You won't tell me what in hell is going on. I had to find out if—"

"I can tell you everything you need to know. You must be patient. Maybe some things I can't tell you right now." He shook his head. "Maybe I . . . ."

August reached down and grabbed him up off the sofa. "Talk to me, and I'll believe you, Bruce. I promise. I've been patient, but lately . . . I don't know what to think."

"You won't believe me if I tell you I don't know who

killed Tommy." He closed his eyes. "Not really."

"What do you mean by, not really?"

"It's complicated."

"Listen, Mr. Curby remembered a man with a dragon tattoo on his arm. He's the one who signed in at the campground with your name or your middle name. Do you know who that man is?"

The fear crept up his spine. *A dragon tattoo.* He pictured that arm extending through the bushes, holding the picture out to Tommy. He could see the outline of that dragon etched on his forearm. Red and blue, breathing fire.

"Did Tommy's killer have a dragon tattoo on his arm?"

"I . . ." He paused. "Yes, I think so. Oh God," he moaned, jerking away from him.

But you always knew, didn't you? That's why you had to be put away.

"Bruce!" August grabbed him again. "Did he have a fucking dragon on his arm, or not? You knew this man. You knew him."

"I didn't see him . . . his face, but I know . . . I mean . . . I know he was there."

"I don't fucking understand." August threw up his hands. "Either you saw him, or you didn't see him."

"I didn't have to see him. I was in his head."

August backed away from him. He was speechless.

"I know you don't understand but . . . God, I can't explain. I have to get out of here." He rushed past August and out the door.

August grabbed his coat and chased after him. There was a light frost on the ground, and it was slippery underfoot. Bruce raced down the road and dashed into some trees. August slipped and slid on the terrain and finally gave up. Bruce had vanished into the night.

When August got back to the house, he punched the wall.

He was so close, and yet, he was more confused than ever. *I didn't have to see him. I was in his head.* What in hell did that mean? Maybe Bruce was insane like Evelyn Monkton had said, and there was no making sense out of anything he said.

Bruce walked along the road, much like he had ten years before. He realized he was still running. He would have kept on going too, but this time . . . No, he couldn't. There was August in the picture now, and he couldn't let anything happen to him. "I love you," he whispered to the night air. "God knows, I've never loved anyone like this in my life-time. He is my everything." He wanted to tell August the truth, or at least what he could remember of it. When he drank, the liquor freed his thoughts, and although it brought fear, at least *he* couldn't touch him when his thoughts were that lucid.

Love, Bruce? Remember what happened the last time you thought about love . . .

"Shut up! Get out of my head. You won't touch him. This time, I'll kill you."

He sang a song in his head to block out the voice until he got to town. He headed right to the liquor store, which mer-cifully hadn't closed yet. He used his last few dollars to buy a cheap bottle of rye, but he was short thirteen cents. The cashier gave him the thirteen cents. He thanked her and left with the bottle tucked under his arm.

He took a couple of swigs before he found the phone booth. He put in the money and dialed with shaking fingers. "Mother," he said, when she answered, "we have to talk. Come quickly and don't say anything. Don't even think it."

He arranged to meet her in an all-night coffee shop on the main street. She arrived a half hour later, bundled up in a big coat, dark circles under her eyes. The first thing she asked him was, "Why'd you have to come back here now, Bruce? You want to stir it all up? It had all died down."

"No, it hadn't. What about the Washington kid?"

"I know nothing about that."

Bruce swallowed. "I know it was a mistake, but maybe listening to you and leaving was a mistake, too. I'm leaving, but you have to promise that August will be safe."

"You can't leave now."

"Yes, I can. He won't come with me. He can't. He can't know."

"You know that I can't guarantee anything if you go, where August is concerned that is. You shouldn't have gotten that involved."

Bruce reached across and grabbed her arm. "This is all on your head, you understand me? And I couldn't help falling in love with him. He's all I've ever wanted, even back when I was a boy, and I saw his picture."

"You're a fool. I'm trying to protect you."

"It's never been me you've protected, and you know it."

"You would be in the institution." Tears sparked her eyes.

"We are talking about murder. We're talking about Tommy and the other boy."

"No. That wasn't—"

"It had to be him. He killed him. I know it. He used him as his teacher and then he got rid of him."

"No." She shook her head. "There was never any body."

"Doesn't mean anything. He could have burned down that abandoned shack with him in it. But I don't understand why he did it this time. Was it just to bring me back here? Goddamn it. Did he know August was trying to find me?"

"He knows everything," she whispered, her eyes wide with fear.

He sighed. "This time it's not an adolescent crush, Mother. I'm not a kid anymore. I love this man. I really love him."

"You can't be with him, you know that."

"All those years he tried to keep me from remembering,

but I remember it all. If he touches August, goes near him, I'll do what I should have done a long time ago, I'll kill myself. It will be the end of him, too."

"No, don't." She sobbed silently, head down. "The sickness is in you, Bruce."

He took her arm. "Come outside with me now." She rose from the table and followed.

When they were outside, Bruce said, "I'm not the sick one. Stop telling me that. I should have gone to the authorities, but I didn't know that he was going to kill Washington. And I didn't know that he was there that night, but I do now. I couldn't connect that man's voice with the boyish laughter. They never went together, but now I understand. He was watching, learning. He gave me the impression that he was chasing me through the woods. No one was chasing me."

"You can't believe that he would . . . ."

"He is following in his footsteps. He intended that all along. He was waiting for the right moment, that's all. Now, with August, when he knows I am finally happy, he decides to fuck up everything for me."

She didn't answer.

"He has to be stopped, Mother. You can't allow him to kill again."

"I'm trying."

For a second, he felt some pity for her. He gave her a quick hug then released her. "Did you lock him in?"

"Yes."

"How did he get out the last time?"

"I don't know. He can hurt you even from there. I have such pain in my head sometimes, migraines. I have to stop the pain somehow."

He held up the bottle. "He can't get to me when I drink."

"I've tried that. It doesn't always work."

"Go home," he said. "Get some sleep."

"Maybe, if you came with me and talked to . . ."

"No. I don't need to go there. We talk all the time. I don't want to look at him."

"Some people would blame me for this. They'd say I did this to him. All those nights in the dark and . . ."

"I don't want to hear this, Mother. You did what you did. You need to live with that." He got up. "I've got to go.

I need to be alone."

August drove around town for hours. Bruce was nowhere in sight. Finally, when he was about to give up, he spotted Desmond outside the police station. He waved and motioned to him to approach. August rolled down the window, and Desmond strode over.

"Hi, handsome," he said. The sun was almost up.

"Hey."

"Looking for something?"

"Bruce Monkton. Seen him?"

"Inside." He hooked his thumb toward the jail. "Drunk as a skunk. Why didn't you tell me he was back and staying with you?"

"Didn't come up."

Desmond was about to say something else, but August cut him off. "I'm coming in. I'll post bail."

"Might as well leave him there. He's out of it, talking crazy. We called his mother. She said she'd come and pick him up in the morning. He's had a lot of problems, August. He's not stable. Where was he when the Washington kid was killed, anywhere around here?"

August shook his head. "I don't think so." He'd promised Bruce that he wouldn't have to go back to his mother's. He couldn't leave him there. "I'll take him tonight, and I promise that I'll get him to come in and talk to you soon."

"Okay. I don't advise it but suit yourself."

August went into the station and posted bail. He was relieved that Desmond had taken off and wasn't there to see him half carry Bruce down the stairs and literally fold him into the front seat. He was babbling, not making much sense, talking to something or someone who wasn't there.

"Hey, baby," he said when August crawled behind the wheel. "You're handsome. Wow! Wish I was sober enough to do something about it."

"Right," August muttered as he started the engine. "Just what I've always dreamed of, some drunk slobbering all over me. Why'd you run off, Bruce? I looked all over hell and gone for you."

"I don't want him to hurt you."

"Who is going to hurt me?" He sat there, staring at him, foot still on the brake.

"Clay," he whispered.

"God damn it, Bruce. Stop talking nonsense. How in the hell can I help you if — "

"He's in the basement." He clutched his forearm so tight it hurt. "Clay is in the basement. I told her to keep him there, but she can't always. He hurts her, hurts her head. Pain is so bad that she had to let him out. I know she should have committed him when he was a kid instead of keeping him in the dark but . . . August, you got to leave here with me now." He pulled on his arm. "Let's just drive, and keep on driving, and . . . He wants you because I love you." He seemed sober suddenly, tears filling his eyes.

"August, don't you understand, I love you."

August's eyes widened. "You . . . you love me?"

"Yes. He won't let that be. I loved Tommy too. It was only a little boy's crush, but it didn't matter. He took him from me, and he'll take you, too."

August sighed. He reached over and touched Bruce's

cheek. His mother had been telling the truth. Bruce was insane. He really thought that he was two people. Oh God, Bruce was a murderer. "You killed Tommy, didn't you?"

"No." He shook his head, sliding back against the car door. "I didn't. I swear."

How much pain was he going to have to endure in this life? He was going to lose him, too, just when . . . Oh God, he loved him. "Bruce, tell me the truth. Damn it, why did you make me . . ."

"Make you what?"

He shook his head. *Why did you make me fall in love with you?* It wouldn't do any good to say that now.

"Forget it."

"August, I don't know what to do. My mother thinks she can control him, protect us both, but she can't."

"You're going to tell this to the police. They'll help you, Bruce. You need to tell them that there is someone in your head telling you to do things. I'll stick by you, baby, I promise. There are doctors." He tried to hold him, but Bruce pushed him away.

"No, please, August, listen to me. I don't need a doctor. He's in my head, but I don't do anything he says. He can't control me. He torments me but right now, I'm drunk, and when I'm drunk, he can't get to me, can't put thoughts in my head, block my memories. I'll tell you what happened, although I swear to God, I didn't know he was there. That laugh, I should have recognized it."

August didn't know what to do. Maybe the best place for him was with his mother, or maybe she was the cause of his psychosis. Maybe he should just take him right back into the police station.

"You hate me, don't you?" he whispered, tears in his eyes.

How could he hate him? He was sick. "No, I don't hate you." August rolled away from the police station and through the dark night. He felt numb as he took the road toward Blood Pond while Bruce shivered in the front seat.

Bruce's mind raced, enduring flashes of the night he watched Tommy Greystone's die seared in his head like a steak on a barbeque.

What's three hundred and eighty thousand times seventeen hundred?
I don't know.
Whoosh.
What's the world's record in feet for the longest come shot?
Please. God, I don't know.
Whoosh.
Come on, Brucie. Want to lose another piece of your beloved? Bet you didn't know this, Tommy. Bruce wanted to fuck you . . . really bad too. Guess that's not going to happen . . .
Whoosh . . .
Whoosh . . .
Guess he's not going to lose his cherry with you. That crazy laugh tingled in his head.

"He kept asking me these insane questions, and I didn't know any of the answers," Bruce said suddenly, keeping his voice cool and controlled. He saw it like a movie, removed from himself.

August looked over at him.

"Every time I didn't know the answer, he hacked off another piece of him. All I could hear were his screams and his cries, and I couldn't do anything. He kept telling me in my head, 'I'm not doing this. You are. You're doing this, Bruce, you're killing him'." Bruce gasped. "August, he was talking to me in my head, but the one who was hurting Tommy, the one with the mask, he was the one asking questions. There were two. Clay was there in my head, but he didn't kill Tommy." He looked at August, who had pulled the car to the side of the road.

August just sat there, staring at him, his face filled with pain.

"You see, baby, this isn't doing any good. It's hurting you."

"I need to hear it," August said between clenched teeth.

"He took it to the bitter end. He tortured and raped him in front of me, and then cut him up into pieces. I was covered with blood, and there was this insane laughing. It was then that I got loose. I was in shock. All I wanted was to get away, and now I know that he wanted me to get away. He never intended to kill me, and now I know why. To kill me was to kill him. But then I think he got rid of the killer, the one he lured there somehow, the one with the dragon on his arm. He was one who killed those other boys all over the state."

August met his eyes. Bruce really believed what he was saying. My God.

"All this time, he was there with this faceless killer in a bizarre mask. I knew he was insane, dangerous, but I never knew him . . . My God, he made the man with the dragon tattoo kill Tommy. He hand-picked him for this serial killer. I'm sure he killed Washington, that he copied the killer's style and . . . God, this time he did it on his own."

"You really believe what you're saying, don't you?"

"Clay is my twin brother, August, but more than that, somehow we can talk to each other in our heads. He's held me hostage in my mind for years. He torments me, and . . ."

"Stop it! Stop it." August pounded his fist on the steering wheel. "I can't listen to this anymore. Get out. Get out of the car." He reached over and pushed open the door.

"Now! I'll give you twenty-four hours to turn yourself in. After that, I'm going to the police."

"Please, August, don't do this. Please, listen to me.

He'll come after you. He knows that I love you and . . ."

August gave him a shove, and Bruce tumbled out of the car. August reached over, slammed the door shut and took off, his tires skidding on the snow-covered road.

Bruce glanced over at Blood Pond. He should have never come back here. August didn't believe anything he said, but then he couldn't blame him. It sounded insane even when he said it. He knew now that Clay had encouraged a serial killer to murder Tommy and made him sign his own name at the campgrounds.

After that night, Clay must have killed the man with the dragon tattoo on his arm. God knows what he'd done with the body. Recently, Clay must have befriended Washington, then killed him too. His mother had lost control. He was getting too strong. Clay had to be stopped, even if it meant that both would have to die.

When August arrived at the summer house, he was in tears. He lowered his head on the steering wheel and sobbed. The horrific details of his brother's death described in a monotone voice by a cold-blooded killer, a killer he'd taken to his bed and fallen in love with, had finally hit him.

The wind howled through the trees. They were going to have a snowstorm. He got out of the car and went into the house. He opened a bottle of whiskey and took it upstairs to his room, along with the family photo album. He looked at the pictures of his brother, smiling, happy. It wasn't fair. None of it was fair. He drank down the whiskey and tried not to think about the pain his brother must have endured as he slowly bled to death that night. *I should have been there. I would have saved you.*

There probably had been a serial killer, a killer with the dragon tattoo on his arm, who'd come to Whitefield and killed his brother, a serial killer who'd already killed several boys in other parts of the state. But August knew now that he'd had an accomplice. Bruce. Bruce had encouraged that man to sign his name as Clay Monkton, for what reason he didn't know, but he was sure of one thing. Bruce had participated in that murder, and that's why he survived, and if anyone killed the man with the dragon tattoo on his arm, it had to have been Bruce himself. Bruce with his sweet smile and passionate kisses. Bruce, who he'd made love to and fucked on this very bed. *God, Tommy, how I've betrayed you.*

The bottle sagged in his hand. His head dropped. His eyes closed. Tomorrow morning he'd call Desmond. He just couldn't face it tonight. Bruce wouldn't have gotten too far if he was trying to make a run for it. He fell asleep on the bed with the photo album lying open across his lap.

A little while later, the violent wind moaning outside muffled the sound of the breaking glass in the kitchen door downstairs.

"Where is he?" Bruce pushed open the front door, almost knocking his mother over.

"Where he always is, of course," she said, chewing her nails.

"You're a liar. You've lost control of him, Mother. He's doing whatever he chooses. We'll go to the police together."

"He's fragile, you know that. He'll never survive it."

"So, you want me to go in his place, is that it?"

"If you plead insanity," she said, "you'll go to some nice place and —"

"And he'll keep on killing because you can't control him anymore!" Bruce screamed. "Stop living in a fantasy world. It's over. I'm not taking the blame for this, for Clay, like when he was a kid, and he did bad things, and you always punished me. You locked him away. Don't you know what living in the dark did to him? You made it worse."

"Your father left me. I was alone. What did you want me to do? He'll be good. I warned him this time."

"He doesn't listen to you anymore. I want to see him. Give me the key," Bruce demanded.

"I . . . I don't know where the key is now." She looked around nervously.

Bruce froze. "Oh no, oh no, Mother, you didn't . . . you didn't let him out, not now, not tonight, when he knows what I intend to do." Bruce raced to the basement door. The lock was off. He yanked open the door and took the steps two at a time. The bed was unmade, the large screen television still flashing some gay pornographic movie.

"Fuck!" Bruce ran back upstairs. His mother cowered in the corner. "Why? Why did you let him out?" He grabbed her, shaking her violently. "Where is he? Where in the fuck is he?"

"August was going to go to the police," she cried. "I couldn't let him do that. If they find him, Bruce, he'd never survive prison, and he doesn't mean it. He doesn't understand. August has to be taken care of."

"You stupid . . ." He picked up the phone and punched in August's phone number. He listened impatiently. It rang and rang. Holding the phone to his ear still, he reached out his hand and said, "Give me the key to your car. Give it to me now!"

She looked around frantically and then grabbed it off the mantel. "What are you going to do?"

He grabbed the key, swore, and handed her the phone. August wasn't answering. "Call the police! Tell them to meet me at Blood Pond. Go on! Do it."

"What are you going to do?" She was running around, waving her arms in the air, hysterical. "What are you going to do, Bruce?" She reached out and clutched onto his arm, sobbing.

"What I should have done a long time ago." He pulled his arm away and glared at her. "If he hurts him, if he lays one hand on August, I'll kill him. Now, do as I fucking told you. Do the right thing for once in your life and call the police!"

Bruce raced out of the house and around back to the garage where his mother kept her car.

Talk to me. Talk to me, you prick. Don't you touch him, Clay, don't hurt him or I swear I'll kill you. I'll kill you.

He got into his mother's car and started it up.

As he drove at breakneck speed toward Blood Pond, Bruce thought about Clay. It had been hard as they grew up to know where one of them began and the other ended. Identical twins, they could be interchanged at school without anyone knowing the difference, and sometimes, when mother felt guilty about keeping Clay out of school, she'd keep Bruce home and put Clay in his place. But then Clay would do bad things, and often Bruce had to take the blame for that.

Mother always said that Clay was the fragile one, which really meant that he was the one she was terrified of. She did what Clay told her for the most part, probably as compensation for her guilt in keeping him locked in the basement. Even when Clay went to the institution, he didn't stay long.

He'd tormented Bruce so much with his voice in his head, Bruce eventually was made to take his place there in order to stop the torment. All the pills, and lonely days in locked cells, while Clay laughed at him. Then finally, his mother agreed just to keep him locked up all the time. And they'd move around so that no one would get suspicious. But Clay was all grown up now. He'd become a man, and his telepathic intimidation had exceeded all expectations. Clay was now the master, and he always wanted everything that Bruce had. And that couldn't be.

August knew that he'd taken a blow to the head and it was bleeding profusely, although he couldn't really see anything. He felt weird. He knew he'd drank a lot before he went to sleep, but it was more than that, like he'd been drugged with something. His limbs felt like lead. He couldn't seem to think straight. When he opened his eyes, he was outside. He saw the blur of trees, and there was a lone figure standing in the distance, out on top of the frozen lake. He was hacking at the ice with something. *Bruce.* August tried to move, but he couldn't. His eyes felt heavy, and they closed again, but he was conscious.

A voice said softly from somewhere, "I tied you to the tree. I apologize for the lack of proper amenities. One should be allowed to die in luxury, don't you think?" A tinkling laugh, soft and light.

"Bruce. Don't. Don't do this."

"I have no choice, my love. You will talk to people about me. That's not a good idea. And no matter how much I love you, you will never truly be mine."

"What we had doesn't mean . . ." He forgot what he wanted to say.

"It was fantastic, lover, but you know, everyone has gotta go. You are beautiful. Usually, I like them younger but, for you," he felt a hand grope him rather clumsily between the leg, "I made an exception. I love your cock. I want to keep it forever."

Silence, then suddenly August heard him say, "Shut up. I'm not listening to you. I don't care what you say, and I'm not afraid of you. I'm more powerful than you. You will be the one to die, not me. I have some special questions this time. I did my homework. Want to play, Brucie Goose?"

August urged himself to stay conscious. He struggled with the ropes around his wrists for a few seconds, but every movement took so much energy. He felt his head drop. He'd lost a lot of blood. He knew he was weak. Hold on, he told himself. Just hold on.

Bruce?

"Clay? Clay, where are you?" Bruce frantically searched the woods. The tips of his fingers were frozen, and only the light of the moon illuminated his path. And, suddenly, it was that night again, and he ran frantically through the woods while someone called his name. Now he knew it had all been in his head. Clay had called him in his mind, never really intending to catch him. He had been running from the shadows.

Bruce stood still at several intervals to rest, bending at the waist. He just listened, trying to feel his brother's presence. He was hiding now, no more taunting. He didn't want to make this easy.

Hurry, he's dying.

Bruce began to run around, his eyes frantically scanning the dark woods. *No, no, please, anything, not him, not him, Clay. I beg you.*

Blood Pond came into view, and in the distance, he could see two silhouettes. He pushed through the icy twigs, slapping them away from him as he trudged forward.

"Clay!"

The figure turned around, his head covered by a dark hood. When Bruce approached, he turned. He had a gun in his hand. Bruce's gaze lit on the gun, then shifted to August who was tied to the tree, slumped over. *Please . . . please . . . please . . . be alive.*

"He's not dead yet. But he will be." Clay gave him a big smile.

"You need help. Let me help you."

"You know what happened last time they put me away. You need to come too."

"Why did you have to kill Tommy? He never did anything to you."

"I didn't do it. You know that. He taught me how. I watched, that's all. He was good. He had no inhibitions."

"The one you made sign his name Clay Monkton, the one with the dragon tattoo on his arm."

"Yes. I heard his thoughts when he came to Whitefield. They called to me. He was going to kill another boy, but I gave him a better suggestion."

"You prick. You chose Tommy. You made him kill Tommy because I cared about him." Bruce's eyes filled with tears.

"Yes. Tommy would have never been yours anyway. He didn't even like cock. He really fought the Dragon Boy when he had his way with him, hated every minute of it. Dragon Boy was a great serial killer, a master, he told me in detail how he killed all those boys up north. His technique was sublime. I've got it down pat. You want to play the game?"

"What happened to him, this killer?" Bruce's gaze stayed on August.

"I buried him in the floor of that old cottage then later, I burnt it down. He was my teacher, but I didn't need him anymore. I'm a fast learner."

Bruce kept advancing, watching the gun. "You killed that other boy a few months ago, too."

"I had to. He was going to go away. He said he was my friend, but when I wanted to get closer to him, he didn't want that. I got what I wanted before I ended his life. He was willing to do everything I wanted. August will only hurt you, Bruce. He'll never love you like I do. Help me; help me to kill him. I'll ask the questions, and see if you can answer them, okay? One bullet for every question you get wrong."

Bruce shook all over. "I beg you, Clay, don't. I love this man. I don't want to play. Kill me instead but leave him alone." *Be strong, Bruce. His life depends on it.*

"Love." He laughed harshly. "You don't know love. If you knew love, you wouldn't have deserted me like you did. You're all I have, Bruce," he moaned, "and I will take what you love every time." He pointed the gun at August. "Now answer the fucking question."

"Okay, okay, easy," Bruce said. "Ask me."

"Are you ready?"

Bruce was ready; he was ready to protect August at all costs. His gaze centered on that gun, and he calculated the distance. He was close enough to propel them both into Blood Pond if he used all his weight.

"When was Whitefield chartered?"

"July Fourth, seventeen seventy-four, you son of bitch!"

Clay's eyes widened as he turned to look at him, and Bruce leaped in the air and tackled him. The gun went off twice and both rolled down the embankment and disappeared into the hole Clay had hacked out in Blood Pond.

CHAPTER EIGHT

When August finally opened his eyes, he heard the constant bleeping of the machines he was connected to. He was alive. He licked his dry lips and reached up to feel a bandage on his head. He coughed a little, and a few minutes later, a nurse walked in. "You're awake." She smiled at him.

He nodded. "Yes. I guess so."

"You've been here for a few days. You lost a lot of blood and were very cold when they found you. You're a lucky young man."

"How did they find me? Who found me?"

"Whitefield Police. They had an anonymous phone call who told them something was happening out at Blood Pond."

"Bruce?" he said.

"I don't know any of the details I'm afraid. You'll have to wait for the police to come and speak to you."

"Can I have a phone? I need to get a hold of Desmond Johnson."

She smiled. "I'll speak to the doctor. You need to rest right now."

Rest? How in hell could he rest? Was Bruce still out there somewhere? It was hard to believe that Bruce had tried to kill him. And if he had, what had stopped him? It sure as hell wasn't him. He'd been out of it, and the last thing he remembered was seeing Bruce hacking ice and then grabbing him between the legs. After that, it was all a fog.

His mind raced as he laid there, but eventually, he fell

back asleep. He saw Bruce's face, sweet, an angel . . . touching him, kissing him. "I love you, Bruce," he said.

"Always believe that. It was real. It was all real."

He woke up with tears on his face. He hastily wiped them away when he saw Desmond walk in the door, dressed in his police uniform. "Hey there." He smiled. "We almost lost you."

"Desmond," August tried to sit up, "what happened? How did you find me? Who called you? Where is Bruce? Is he all right?"

"Whoa, calm down there, August." He placed a hand on his shoulder and eased him back down. "We don't know everything yet. And I'm hoping that you can fill in some blanks. We're not sure who called in, but it might have been Mrs. Monkton. Luckily, it was right after you were taken up there. We went by her house to find out if she'd heard anything from her son, and she was gone."

"Gone?"

"Yep. She just took off, left just about everything. Probably just packed a suitcase. And we're not even sure how she got out of town yet. We found her car down by Blood Pond. Who took you down there, August?" He pulled up a chair. "Walk me through it."

"I picked Bruce up at the police station, as you know."

"We spoke. I remember. Hate to say I told you so but . . . I did say to leave him there."

"I know. Live and learn. Anyway, Bruce seemed scared of his mother. He didn't want to go near her." August took a breath. "He was really wasted. He was talking nonsense. Couldn't make out much of what he said.

I think he's . . . he thinks he's two people, Desmond."

"Is that so? Do you think he killed the Washington kid?"

"I hope not. I mean, I know he was in New Hampshire during that time, but I don't think he was here in town."

"Not that I recall. Did he kill Tommy?"

"I found a book from July two-thousand and nine. The Curbys gave it to me. There's a signature in there, a Clay Monkton. I think, from what Bruce told me, that he was the serial killer police were looking for."

"Those murders upstate?"

"Yeah. I think this guy killed Tommy, but that Bruce was a . . ." He paused.

"He was in on it?"

August closed his eyes. "It's so hard for me to say this. Part of me can't even imagine it. Part of me . . ."

"You and Bruce?" Desmond lifted an eyebrow.

August nodded miserably.

Desmond was quiet a moment. "Sorry, man. Okay, so you had a fight. What then?"

"I kicked him out of the car, said I was going to turn him in. He kept pleading with me to listen to him." August shook his head. "I went home. I was feeling bad. I drank more than I should have, and I fell asleep. Next thing I know, I was tied to a tree out at Blood Pond, and Bruce was hacking at the ice with something. I don't remember much more."

"The alcohol combined with the blow to the head made you groggy. You also inhaled some ether. He put you out and then took you to Blood Pond. We think he must have taken his mother's car. We've dusted it for fingerprints and dusted your house. We found the same prints. Bruce Monkton was driving that car."

August bit his bottom lip.

"We figure the mother felt guilty and called it in. She's probably known about her son's psychiatric problems for a long time. Family has had an erratic history from what we understand. Moved from place to place, and Bruce was in a facility back in Boston when he was kid. Multiple personality disorder. Doctor who treated him said he heard a voice in his head all the time."

August closed his eyes.

"What happened to Bruce? Is he in custody?"

"No. When we got there, we only found you. We think that instead of shooting you, he turned the gun on himself. We didn't find the weapon, but we think the gun, and Bruce, may be at the bottom of the lake. There was a huge hole punched through the ice and some breakage around the hole like someone fell. There was blood, too."

"Oh, God."

Desmond stood up. "Police divers were brought in. They searched the surface of the pond, but it's too cold to dive into it this time of year. When they got to about ten feet, they had to stop. Blood Pond is about twenty feet in the middle. We'll have to wait until spring to see what we turn up." He leaned over his bed. "Just one thing, August."

"Yeah?" He looked off into the distance for a moment, sadness filling him.

"Do you think that Bruce could have had someone else with him the other night when he took you out there?"

"What do you mean?" August looked at him. "You don't think he was alone?"

Desmond looked uncertain. "Just speculating. We found no traces of blood in the car, and you were bleeding quite a bit. We can't figure out how he got you to Blood Pond unless someone else took you there. Also, the trauma to the ice is bigger than one man would make. When you noticed him out on the ice punching that hole did you happen to see someone else, hear someone?"

"No," August replied, narrowing his eyes. "I only saw him, and it was from quite a distance."

"Also, we found two sets of tracks in the snow, right in front of the tree where you were tied up. One was a pair of boots, about size nine, nine and half, and the other tracks were made by running shoes of some kind, same size."

"Running shoes? Bruce had on running shoes. He never did get around to buying boots."

Desmond nodded. "We found those tracks again, going off in the other direction. Seems like they were weighed down by something, they're deeper in the snow, and erratic kind of. Then they get to the road, and they disappear."

August was sitting up again. "Tracks made by the running shoes or the boots?"

"Running shoes," he said. "And there was blood, quite a bit. If there was a second person there, we think whoever it was might have gotten a ride on the road."

"Could be the mother. Her car was there."

He nodded. "Given the running shoes, the tracks were probably Bruce's, but it's strange. Like I said, it seemed like he'd put on a few pounds. The tracks are far deeper."

"Two," August said.

"What?"

"What if Bruce was telling the truth? What if there are two of them?"

"Twins, you mean?" August nodded.

"Anything is possible. Twin killers."

"What if only one of them is a killer?"

"August, I know it's wishful thinking but . . ."

"Find the birth record for Bruce Monkton. Find out if there were two."

Desmond nodded. "Okay. You rest. I'll see what I can do."

After Desmond left, August lay there thinking of all the things Bruce had told him. It was hard to sort out. But he'd seen someone who looked like Bruce that day in town, and yet Bruce was at his house the whole time. Evelyn Monkton seemed nervous when he'd visited her as if she didn't want him to go into the house. How could Bruce have killed Washington unless he'd been in Whitefield or Lancaster at the time? Desmond didn't remember seeing Bruce at all in town. Why would he come back here specifically to kill Washington?

Why wasn't he dead? That was the biggest question.

If Bruce had gone to all that trouble to take him out to Blood Pond, to stop him from talking to the police, he should be dead now. What in hell had happened out there?

He wanted out of this hospital. Something just wasn't right. It wasn't right at all.

"How long you going to keep me tied up like this, Bruce?"

"Until I decide what to do with you. Now shut up."

"You should have let me drown in the pond."

"Yes, I know," he said softly, sliding down on the floor of the old barn. "But I couldn't do it. I tried."

"You're guilty of everything I've done. They're looking for us now, hunting us."

Bruce looked over at Clay. With the same hair and same eyes, he might have been looking at himself, except there was something else in Clay's eyes, something crazed. *Insanity.*

"You should call Mommy. She wouldn't approve of what you're doing to me."

"I know, but I don't give a fuck. Mother can't protect you anymore, Clay. That's over. I have to take control of you now. I can't keep letting you do whatever you want . . . killing people."

"If I go to prison—"

"You won't. They'll lock you into some hospital somewhere like before."

"And you'll be there with me, every single day unless you

kill me. So, do it," he urged. "Do it, brother. I'm telling you, once you get the taste for it, hmm, the taste is sweet. You know I never knew how much August and Tommy looked alike."

"Shut up," Bruce snapped. "Don't even say his name. And don't talk about what you did. I know all about it."

"He's probably dead, your lover. You know, even big tough, macho ex-cops die of hypothermia. He was bleeding all over."

"He's not dead. Shut the fuck up."

"There are rats in here, you know."

"Ignore them."

"I don't like rats. There were rats in that basement in Boston. And it was cold like here."

He didn't answer. He'd found an old barn off the main road. It was little more than a shell. They had been here for almost three days now.

"I watched you that night."

"What night?" He closed his eyes. He was frozen, starved, and he had a bullet lodged in his thigh. It hurt like hell.

"One night at his house at the lake. I watched through the window. I watched you love him. I could feel it almost, the pleasure when he was inside you. I feel you. You are like me."

Bruce scrambled over, reached over and placed a hand around his brother's throat. "I am nothing like you," he growled.

Clay laughed then choked. "That's it, that's it." Bruce let him go.

"The only way to get free is to kill me, Bruce. Do it. No one would blame you. All these years, psychologically tied to me, feeling my insanity; and mother, because she thought I was the fragile one, making you take the blame for everything." He laughed. "But I am the strong one. You know that now, don't you? You better kill me because the first chance I get, I'll turn on you. Do you remember when I skinned that—"

"Shut up! That was disgusting, and you're disgusting. Shut up. Don't talk anymore."

"Hush, little baby, don't say a word," he started to sing.

Bruce waited until Clay fell asleep. He was feeling weak, dizzy. It might have been from the blood loss. He had to do something. He pulled out the cell phone he'd found in the glove compartment of his mother's car. He glanced around the old barn. They were off the main road. Maybe he wouldn't get a signal. He turned it on. It searched, and finally, there it was. He had very few choices now. He needed medical attention. And Clay had to be locked up. It didn't matter where they put him. Maybe he could find a way to disconnect from him. He dialed the number and let it ring. "Please answer."

It was probably a mistake, but he had to know. He had to know.

"Hello?"

"August?"

There was silence then, "Oh God, Bruce, where are you?"

Silent tears rained down his face. "Are you all right? Are you all right, baby?"

"I'm okay. Where are you, Bruce? The police are looking for you."

"I know. I couldn't do it. I couldn't kill him." Silence again. "I know you think I'm insane but—"

"No. I know there are two of you. You have a twin named Clay, only he's been hidden. Bruce, you need to stop protecting him. He needs help. He's a killer."

"You don't understand," he said. "We have this connection. He can read my thoughts, I can read his. Last time he was put away, he tormented me. He almost drove me in-

133

sane. He'll never let me go. The only thing to do is for both of us to die. I can't kill him. I tried. It's not in me."

"Where are you? Tell me. I'll come to you."

"No. I don't want you anywhere near him. I thought when we went into Blood Pond, it was the end, but I guess the will to survive is strong. And I pulled him out. I carried him to the road. Damn it," he sobbed, "I should have left him to die."

"He's your brother," August said on the other end.

"Let me help you. I love you."

Bruce began to sob. *He loves me. August loves me.*

"Bruce, where are you?"

He wiped his face on his sleeve. "I'm about thirty miles north of Lancaster, on a road called Dustin Mills. It's an old abandoned barn. August, I've been shot."

"Oh my God, okay. Hold on. I'm coming. Where is Clay?"

"I've tied him up. He's not going anywhere. Hurry," he breathed. Bruce felt weak all of sudden. His world started to spin. His head slumped forward, and the cell phone dropped into his lap.

August threw blankets and a first aid kit into the back seat of his car. He loaded his pistol, shoved some extra bullets into his coat pocket, and got behind the wheel of his car. He didn't call Desmond, and he felt torn as he drove. Desmond didn't even know that August had checked himself out of the hospital yet. He just couldn't lie there anymore, and as soon as Desmond had told him about the birth certificate, August was on the move. He knew Bruce had to be in trouble, and he was hoping he'd call him.

Desmond had been upfront with him the last two days, telling him how Mrs. Monkton had covered up the fact that she'd had two sons. "Looks to me like she kept one of them locked up all the time. Basement door had a padlock on it, and there was a bed and a television down there. If the kid started out nuts, you can imagine how he ended up after all that."

"Oh my God," August replied, "how could she do such a thing?"

"I think he was out of control, and maybe she thought she was doing what was best for him. One of those boys was in the hospital, but given that they are identical, we can't determine which one. In the basement of the house here in town, we found DVDs of hard-core gay porn and clippings of articles from newspapers and the internet on serial killers, especially the cases in New Hampshire a while back. "I'm pretty sure he was involved with the murder of the Washington kid, and even your little brother. Now, the question is where in the hell is he? Is he with his mother, or is he with Bruce? We don't even know which one is still alive."

August drove out of town a little too fast, reminding himself to slow down so he didn't get stopped by the police. It was the last thing he needed. He wasn't sure what to do once he got there, but he knew he needed to help Bruce. Together, maybe they could bring Clay to the police. He tried to stop himself from feeling guilty. Maybe he should have trusted Bruce more, but then Bruce had been so confused himself.

He'd been driving for about forty minutes, convinced that he now understood what was going on. When he saw the sign, he almost missed it. He took the turn-off down the dark road, and there in the middle of the field was the abandoned barn. He pulled the car over to the side of the ditch, took out his gun, and began to trudge across the snowy field. He spotted an old truck parked sideways beside a structure that looked like it was about to cave in. "Bruce?"

he called out, his boots sinking into the soggy ground.

The moon grinned overhead. He tightened his grip on the gun in his hand. That doubt he'd had before crept back up his spine.

"I'm here, baby," a voice called out.

There was movement at the barn door. The wind rocked it a little, and it squeaked on its rusty hinges. August narrowed his eyes. "Come out where I can see you."

"I love you, August," he said softly. He stood a few feet away now, his eyes shining. "Aren't you going to kiss me?"

"I thought you were wounded." August stiffened, his finger caressing the trigger.

"I'm okay," he said, "just a flesh wound. I'm okay now that you're here with me."

He moved forward, his arms open. August raised the gun, and it trembled in his hand. He saw the glint of steel, glanced down at the man's feet, then raised the gun and fired.

"August! August!"

Another figure stumbled around the door, hobbling on one leg as August leaned down to check the pulse of the one on the ground. It was uncanny. They were identical. It felt like he was looking down into Bruce's face.

"Bruce!" He ran over and pulled him into his arms. "Don't look."

"Are you all right?" Bruce buried his face in August's coat.

"Yes," August said.

"How did you know?"

"The boots." August looked down at Bruce's running shoes for reassurance. He kissed the top of his head and held him for a moment. "I'm sorry. I had no choice. He had a knife."

"It was meant to be. Is he . . ."

"Yes. Come on, I need to call the police, and an ambulance. I have to get you to the hospital. How did he get loose?"

"I passed out. I guess I didn't tie him tight enough.

He was probably loose all along. August," he said while August pulled out his phone, "I don't think this is going to be easy for me. I may need to see someone."

August hugged his shoulders. "We'll see someone together, okay?"

Bruce kissed him. "Okay."

Epilogue

Five years later

Nothing had been easy for the few months that followed Clay Monkton's' death. Bruce was treated in hospital and subjected to rigorous questioning by the police. Finally, to August's relief, he was cleared of all suspicion. His mother, Evelyn Monkton, was prosecuted for child abuse and withholding of evidence and was serving a seven-year term in New Hampshire State Prison for Women in Goffstown.

Bruce started therapy in Manchester and went back to school. He took a degree in business and became interested in marketing. He started his own company and travelled all over the state of New Hampshire as a marketing consultant. August went back to the Manchester homicide squad and attended a bereavement group for relatives of murder victims off and on. They bought a nice little house in Manchester, and it finally felt like they were putting their demons to rest.

Bruce still got panicky for little reason, but an occasional Alprazolam usually calmed him down. August was off the medication for depression completely and had found peace. They had each other to get them through the bad dreams, which came less and less as time went on.

One weekend, August came to join Bruce in Whitefield. He'd been there for a week, giving a training session to a new company. After some persuasion, Bruce agreed to go with him to the cemetery. August wanted to visit Tommy's and his mother's graves.

August stood in front of his brother's gravestone, hand in hand with Bruce, early in that warm July evening. He said his goodbyes and turned to Bruce. "Do you want to visit Clay's grave?"

Bruce shook his head. "No."

"I don't mind."

"I know you don't mind," he said tensely. "I just don't want to."

"Bruce," August looked into his eyes, "he was sick. And your mother made it worse, hiding him away, keeping him locked up like that. None of this is your fault. I don't blame you for Tommy. You know that now, I hope."

He nodded, squeezing August's hand. "I know, baby. It's tough for me. That's all."

Clay's grave was a little way away from Tommy's in a shaded area, under a tree. He'd never been to it. This was the first time. He'd been here all week giving training to the new marketing firm, and he hadn't thought once of going to Clay's grave.

Finally, after some coaxing by August to face his fears, he walked steadily over to the gravestone with its simple engraving. Just his name with the date of birth was written there. He was finally free of him. There were no more voices in his head. "You can't talk to me from the grave, can you, brother?"

"They're both at peace now." August turned him around. "Let's leave them that way. Now," he grinned, pulling Bruce out of the graveyard, "how about I give you your surprise?"

"Which is?"

"I sprang for a room in the most luxurious hotel in town."

Bruce grinned. "You mean the Mountain View House?"

"I took the liberty of getting us a room for your last night here in Whitefield."

"I love you." Bruce kissed his jaw.

"You better. Cost me a bundle."

"Gonna' frisk me, officer?"

August raised his eyebrows up and down a few times, making Bruce laugh as they got into the car.

They wasted no time checking in. They had a beautiful room with a great view facing the Presidential Range. It sure beat the inn he'd been staying in all week.

"Look at that," August was saying, pointing at something out the window.

All Bruce could see was the gorgeous man standing in front of him, this man who'd changed his entire life, and finally given him what he thought he'd never have. He went up behind him and wrapped his arms around his slim waist. "Never mind that," he growled. "I've missed you, baby. I want to fuck."

August laughed that soft, husky laugh that came out when he was feeling frisky himself, and Bruce pulled his own t-shirt over his head and threw it on the floor. Then he reached down and unzipped his jeans, pressing his erection against August's hip.

"Are you going to strip me right in the window where everyone can see?"

"Yeah. I want everyone to see what a hunk I have, and then after they get to see you naked, I'm going to take you right here and now, fuck you so hard and so . . . mmm . . . August, I love you." He pushed August's jeans down off his hips and lifted his sex out of his underwear. "God, you're so hard, just like I like it." Bruce stroked August's cock in even jerks while one hand began to play with his left nipple. He kissed August's neck, and August let his head fall back on his shoulder.

Bruce's hand left his cock and pulled his briefs off. They

fell to his ankles. The hand on August's nipple moved down to fondle his balls now, and the other moved between his hard, round ass, seeking out his anus with his finger.

August grunted as Bruce's finger entered him, and the hand massaging his balls moved back up to cuff his cock a little. "Say you're mine," Bruce urged.

"I'm yours," he grunted.

Bruce released him. "Get on the bed. I've got a treat for you."

August laughed. "Shit, you mean that was just the appetizer?"

"Oh yeah," he said, lube and condoms in hand. He crawled onto the bed with him. "You wait until you see the main course. I want to play with your body all night long." Bruce licked his nipples and then worked some scented oil into them. "You're so sexy," he whispered. "Your nipples are so hard. They taste like candy."

"You've been drinking."

"Not a drop."

August smiled then grunted as one of his legs went up over Bruce's shoulder. He lifted a vibrating dildo in one hand and smeared it with lube. "Just to open you up." He kissed his lips and then nibbled all the way down his chest.

"That will do it."

Bruce teased his anus a little more then pushed the dildo up inside of him.

August grunted and then moaned a little, his hips working as Bruce fucked him with it. He loved to watch August get off, watch his face, his cock bounce, and his balls tighten. He'd always wanted a little kink, and August was always willing to let him have it. "Move your hips more," he urged, feeling his cock pulse. "Shit, August, I'm going to come just watching you."

"Leave it in," he urged. "Get on all fours. I'll fuck you

now."

Bruce eagerly turned around on the bed. The dildo pulsed inside August as his cock took possession of Bruce's ass. He pumped and pumped until they both cried out their release, August's hand squeezing Bruce's softening dick. They curled up together on the bed, and Bruce kissed him passionately. "I love your mouth. I love you."

"Mmm, good," he said, the dildo finally going silent.

Bruce moved down and began to suck his cock, watching it slowly get hard again.

"You trying to kill me." He eyed him with a smile.

His cock hardened again, Bruce began to lube himself. "Never. I want to ride it. This time, I'm on top, okay?"

August put himself into position, lifting his hips, and Bruce straddled him. As Bruce moved up and down on August's cock, he watched his lover's face. Bruce knew they'd be together forever. They'd been through too much.

He'd never let August go, ever.

Later that night, they sat eating a cold supper and drinking chilled lemonade. Both had sworn off drinking altogether since they'd left this town. Bruce had leaned over and was just feeding August a shrimp dipped in cocktail sauce when August's cell phone rang.

"Don't answer it," Bruce pleaded. "Please, baby."

"I'm sorry, sweetie, I got to," he said. "It could be an emergency. Hold that thought."

"Or hold that shrimp," Bruce muttered comically.

August laughed and went over to pick up his phone off the night table. "Greystone here."

Bruce watched him from where he sat at the table, sipping his drink. *Beautiful. What a big gorgeous man he is. My man.*

"Yes. When?" August's face went dark. "Where?"

He paused. "Where did you say? Are you sure? I see. Okay.

Don't let anyone touch anything until I get there."

Bruce jumped to his feet. "No, can't they do without you for one night? I swear to God that sometimes they think you're the only detective on the Manchester police force. We don't have to go back there tonight, do we? Damn it, August," he whined, "we just checked in."

August stared straight ahead as if he hadn't heard a word Bruce said. "There's no need to pack," August said softly. "That was the police in Lancaster." He turned to look at Bruce. "A fifteen-year-old boy went missing from Whitefield two days ago. They just found his head . . . at the bottom of Blood Pond."

You may also enjoy the following from eXtasy Books Inc:

Blood Pond Resurfacing
D.J. Manly

Excerpt

The sun had already risen when August drove around the lake back toward town, and despite the sun, the sky looked doubtful about what direction it would take for the remainder of the day. He'd hung around until forensics finished up, and he'd spoken to the girls' parents, who frankly seemed more concerned about their daughters hanging out together than they did about a boy's head being in the pond. People were strange.

As he pulled into town, he spotted Alice Comeau standing outside the town diner. He checked his watch. Place wouldn't open for a little while yet.

Alice, or Al, as she was more commonly called, was working homicide when he returned to the job four years ago. They'd collaborated on a few cases. Then she got interested in the scientific end of things and ended up going back to school. Now she worked forensics. She was an attractive woman around thirty, athletic and tough, with dark wavy hair. She was one hell of a cop too, but she didn't have much luck with men. She'd already been divorced twice. It was a running joke in the department.

When Alice saw him, she waved.

He pulled over to the curb and grinned at her. "Hungry?"

"When in the hell is breakfast in this one-horse town anyway?" She grinned at him then looked back at the diner.

"Opens at eight, Al, usually, if you're lucky."

"Hell, another hour. I'm starved."

"Get in," he said. "I'll give you some gum to chew."

She walked around and got into the passenger side, laughing. "Want a smoke?"

"Yeah, I want a smoke, but I quit, remember?"

"Wish I could. How did you do it?

"I suffered," he replied.

"I won't smoke," she said, stuffing her pack back into the pocket of her windbreaker.

"It's okay. Open the window. It won't bother me."

She shook her head. "Trying to kill me off, eh, Gus? Forget it; I'll suffer, too." She paused then gave him a meaningful look. "How are you doing anyway?"

"I'm doing," he sighed, laying his head back against the headrest. He was tired, but he knew even if he went back to the hotel, he wouldn't be able to sleep.

She reached out and stroked his hair for a second then quickly withdrew. "If you asked to be taken off this case, no one would blame you, you know?"

He lifted his head, peering at her. "Funny, Bruce practically said the same thing a little while ago. I don't want to be off this case."

"Okay."

"Look, there is no evidence that Clay killed his accomplice. He might have told Bruce that, but it doesn't mean it was true."

"How is Bruce?" She looked out the passenger window.

He almost expected her to spit when she said his name. She'd never liked him, although he knew she tried hard to hide it. "Fine."

That bitch hates me. She wants you between her thighs, that's why.

He hated it when Bruce talked like that. Bruce had told him that one night after they'd come home from a retirement party for one of the big brass in the department. It was the first time he'd met Alice. August didn't believe it for a minute, and it really bothered him how possessive and jealous Bruce could get. Bruce was frail in his own way and insecure, and so usually August put it down to that and let it go.

"Johnson told me he was in town all week," Alice said, bringing August back to the present.

"Who?"

"Bruce."

"A lot of people were in this town all week, Al." He gave her a meaningful look.

"I know but ... given his connection with all this stuff ..." She sighed. "You do know that he's being considered a suspect."

"A suspect? That's ridiculous."

"Desmond Johnson told me. Bruce shouldn't leave town just yet."

"You've got to be fucking kidding me."

She put up a hand. "Don't shoot the messenger. If you ask me, Desmond Johnson is a bit of a Rambo, not to mention that he's in love with you. That doesn't help."

August's mouth dropped open.

"Oh, don't act so surprised, August. It's obvious that you banged the poor salivating dope back at the academy. You did go to the academy together, didn't you?"

August made a face. "Ancient history."

"For you, maybe."

"I need to talk to him about Bruce. He's way out of line."

"Look, August, you know that usually, I've got your back. Hell, we were partners. But, on this one, I'm afraid I agree with him."

"What? I can't believe you. Bruce was cleared of everything after his brother was shot."

She nodded quietly. "His mother still up in the pen doing time?"

"Yeah."

"Does Bruce see her?"

"No. He wants nothing to do with her."

"It was a strange case. Clay was kept in the basement because he was unstable, but his mother said he could cause her to have headaches if she didn't do as he said. Personally, I never bought that one. Even Bruce claimed that Clay could speak to him in his mind."

"There have been a lot of studies on identical twins, Al. Anything is possible."

"Why did the mother protect the bad one? Why didn't she admit him to the hospital? She claims to this day that Bruce was the sick one, not Clay."

"She wants revenge against Bruce for testifying against her, that's all."

"Um . . ."

"Okay, what? Out with it."

"Nothing. Just Bruce hung out with your brother, fell for him, but Tommy was straight, not interested, and suddenly, his twin emerges from the basement, lures a serial killer here and takes them both hostage? The killer never touches Bruce though, not to mention that Bruce takes off and leaves town when he escapes instead of going to the police."

August looked at her. "It looks like you've spent some time reading the files. Bruce was in shock, terrified."

"But he knew Clay was involved."

"Not at the time. He was confused."

"Tell me what you remember after Clay took you to Blood Pond."

"What for?"

"Just to appease me."

"Okay." He sighed. "Clay came to my house, knocked me

out and took me to Blood Pond. He tied me to a tree, and I assume meant to kill me. He almost did. If it hadn't been for Bruce, I'd be dead. He went there to Blood Pond and tackled Clay. They fell into the pond and then, instead of leaving Clay, Bruce pulled him out. He'd been shot."

"How did Clay get you to Blood Pond alone? I've seen Bruce. He and Clay must have been around the same size."

August nodded.

"You're a big guy, August, tall, muscular. Do you think someone of that stature could have carried you to Blood Pond? Was there ever a vehicle found?"

"What are you saying?"

"I'm saying I doubt he could have done it alone."

"So, Bruce helped him? Is that what you are trying to say? Al, if Bruce wanted me dead, don't you think he would have found a way to do it by now? We sleep in the same bed for Christ's sake."

"I never said that Bruce wanted you dead. I truly think he loves you. But Bruce and Clay had an unusual bond, August. I think it was wrapped up all too neatly. After Bruce called you, after he'd supposedly stopped Clay from killing you, you went to find them, right?"

"Yeah."

"Someone came out of the barn when you got there, and you knew it was Clay."

"He was wearing boots."

"Were they dressed exactly alike? The twins?"

"Similar. Jeans, Clay had a coat. Bruce was wearing a couple of layers of clothes. He didn't own a coat, and he had on running shoes."

"Other than that, could you tell them apart? Was it dark?"

"Fairly dark; it was the middle of winter, early evening." He hesitated. He knew where she was going.

Al looked at him. "August . . ." She touched his hand, her voice growing softer as she met his gaze. "Did you ever think that maybe you shot the wrong twin?"

ABOUT THE AUTHOR

I write not only for my own pleasure but for the pleasure of my readers. I can't remember a time in my life when I haven't written and told stories. When I'm not writing, I'm dreaming about writing, doing something wild and adventurous, or trying to make the world a better and more open-minded place to live in. I adore beautiful men, and I know I'm not alone in this! Eroticism between consenting adults, in all its many forms, is the icing on the cake of life!

D.J. has published well over two hundred novels/novellas and is a well-seasoned writer.